Brax held his breath. His gun hand was twitching. He uncurled his trigger finger and flexed it. Soon his legs would ache; he had been crouching for many minutes and they were stiff. The man glided past. Brax could see the brocade on the band of his sombrero, the hat tied back over his shoulders to make for a smaller target. Brax had seen enough.

"Tip one more toe and I'll bring you down, boy."

# SLICKROCK RECKONING

## RANDOLPH NEWMAN

*A Novel Idea*
610 W. Main St.
Leesburg, FL 34748
(352) 326-8558

**CHARTER**
NEW YORK

A DIVISION OF CHARTER COMMUNICATIONS INC.
A GROSSET & DUNLAP COMPANY

**51 Madison Avenue
New York, New York 10010**

## SLICKROCK RECKONING

An ACE CHARTER Original


First Ace Charter Printing August, 1982


Published simultaneously in Canada
Manufactured in the United States of America

2  4  6  8  0  9  7  5  3  1

# SLICKROCK
# RECKONING

# One

Four years' worth of his life jingled in Don Braxton's pockets and it wouldn't buy a white girl for an hour.

The massive iron gate clanged shut behind him. He stood for a moment, filling his lungs with searing desert air. Just as goddamn hot on this side of the wall as inside. He smiled and strolled down Prison Hill into Yuma.

When they gave Braxton two to five he figured he'd be out in eighteen months. He figured wrong. Now he looked over his shoulder at the looming fortress of Yuma Territorial, pictured the rows of white crosses in the prison graveyard. He turned to the dusty sun-bleached alleys of the town below. There really wasn't room for joy, only relief.

A drink is high on the list of a man who's had nothing but kitchen-peelings moonshine—and precious little of that—for four years. Braxton made straight for the nearest watering hole, a squat two-story frame house with large overhanging eaves that shaded the doors and windows. He squinted in the glare thrown by the brilliantly whitewashed siding. A black sign carved in the shape of a bull hung over the front door.

1

The bottom floor, judging from the noise and the smell, was the saloon. Sweaty women leaning out of the upper windows left no doubt about the purpose of the rooms above.

He walked into a fog of sweat, smoke, and liquor. Wet gauze hung over the open windows so that hot air pushed through by an obliging breeze would cool down as it sucked the water from the fabric. But no friendly wind blew here, and the air was rank enough to make him cough. Still, it wasn't much next to the stench of the punishment cells.

Braxton made it halfway to the bar before a new smell intruded, faint but conspicuous. A woman and her perfumes.

"You want company tonight." It was a statement, not a question from this small dark girl.

Don Braxton looked her over. Young, Mexican, with large heart-melting brown eyes and jet-black waist-length hair. Yes, he did want company tonight.

On the other side of the room the bar propped up a pudgy young man with dull eyes. The drinker nudged his two companions. The three of them were strangers here, they had just stepped off the train. The had drunk their way through the entire Southern Pacific leg of the journey, but the stout youth was careful. Careful to keep his face turned away while the others watched Braxton reach into his pocket and show the girl his fortune.

"It ain't much," Braxton said.

"No, Cowboy," Small, good teeth flashed glossy white in the deep olive-brown of her face. "It is not much."

"And I . . . I was hoping to buy a bottle."

She looked him up and down and her smile almost turned to a giggle. He was rawboned and rangy, lean from a prison diet that was supposed to be better than most. A once luxurious black mane was thinning on top and streaked with gray. A thick handlebar flowed off his lips, spilling over his chin. His cheeks sported a fresh shave but they were sunken, and his narrow head and longish nose lent him a sad look. This was a striking face; there was strength, and there were kind-looking crow's-feet and flashing smile lines.

The girl looked into his deeply set steel-blue eyes, then to the money he held in his scarred and callused hand. "It will do, friend."

"My friends call me Brax."

"And mine, Rosa."

From the bar three pairs of eyes followed them up the rickety stairs. Rosa led him to a small room furnished with a cheap metal frame bed. A mesquite highchair served as a nightstand. On the tray of the highchair stood a candle. She lit it and low-grade tallow flickered into lazy streams of oily smoke.

Sundown brought little relief from the leaden heat. Brax threw the window wide but no breeze stirred the gossamer drapes. He stared at the lights of town, murky through the curtain. She sat on the bed. Young, pretty, schoolgirlish. Totally at ease. Brax wished he could drift back to those intoxicating spring days when he could still feel wonder. Instead he felt the blood throbbing through his temples. "I undress you," she said, and reached for his shirt buttons.

But it was no good. His breath was coming up short; soon he'd be fighting for air. The old fear was back. He pushed her hand away, hoping he wasn't too rough.

"Can such a big rugged man be shy?"

Brax managed a smile which unleashed her windchime laughter. She got up on tiptoes and kissed him. He did not resist.

"You are tense, no? I rub you."

"I'm all right." Brax looked at the bottle he held. Where had it come from?

"Then I undress for you." She blew out the candle. Moonbeams flooded the room. Brax stood near the highchair and watched. She undid the string that held her billowy cotton blouse, then slipped out of the long brocaded skirt. Her flesh in the moonlight made him queasy.

He had to sort this thing out. A little more whisky maybe. It was now, this slim tawny young body, not then; this had nothing to do with that dank morning. He had to throw that aside, beat the memories back. He had to do it, he *was* doing it. He felt himself stirring. And then he knew it was going to be all right.

For a time, in the heat of the Arizona night, things were good again and Don Braxton was back among the living.


Paradise, Vicente Alvarez knew, was a few pesos away. He'd drunk in worse places, but couldn't remember when. No air fanned the tobacco haze or lifted the steam of drying sweat. Vicente had traveled long and hard to see his woman, but after so many months apart another night wouldn't matter. The weeks on the trail demanded a bottle of tequila and a tub of cool water.

He shouldered his way through the room to the counter where a lone bartender did his best to keep up with the clamoring crowd. He found leaning-space against the bar and waited his turn, grateful to be out of the saddle. Today had been the longest, hottest day of all.

Vicente rubbed shoulders with a chubby vacant-looking youth, one of three well-armed strangers; he took them in with dark narrow-set eyes and absently fingered his pencil-thin moustache. The barkeep slammed a fresh bottle of whisky on the counter in front of them, mopped his brow and disappeared again. In spite of the heat, these men wore buckskins and dusters. High-country clothing. Shootists, judging from the crossdraw holster on one and the brace of Colts on another. Vicente eavesdropped, but lost interest when the bartender showed with his tequila. All Vicente wanted was to get out of there, soak his weary frame, and feel like a human being again.


In the little room upstairs the bottle lay on its side under the bed. Cheap rye whisky, but next to Prison Hill rotgut it was like ten-year-old Kentucky bourbon. Brax slept while the young whore went through the pockets of his trousers.

She looked at the man in the moonlight. She'd seen how the liquor had waxed his eyes, but his snore wasn't the dead wheeze of a drunk. He was gentle for one in such need. The kind eyes and smile hid a deep unhappiness.

The pockets were empty. Rosa put his pants back on the highchair next to his gunbelt and made to light the candle but the matches slipped from her fingers and were lost in the darkness. She went down on hands and knees and felt for them. She found the matches, stood up facing the window, and saw moonlight flash from the end of the rifle barrel.

The muzzle of a carbine nudged aside the curtain. The girl watched the face outside as the gun was trained on the sleeping man. The gunman cocked the rifle with a sound that echoed through the room. Brax stirred but did not waken. The man in the window raised his head and looked directly at Rosa. Her throat tightened, but a shriek escaped. Without knowing why she threw herself onto the bed, onto Brax. A single shot rang out and she slid dead to the floor.

Brax's eyes were wide open and the Colt was in his hand before the man could shove another cartridge into the chamber. Instinct guided his first shot, but anger jerked back the hammer and fired again. The carbine clattered to the landing, the man's hands went to the oozing holes in his chest, and he fell. The railing screeched with tearing wood as the body plunged ten feet to the dust and the horse droppings of the street.

Vicente was on his way out when the three shots rang out. A few drinkers stepped outside for a look. Gunfire was common in Yuma, but a killing was always an event. When the dead man was spotted the saloon belched forth its sweat-soaked crowd.

A man who spent the previous night in Yuma Territorial doesn't stick around to explain a dead whore in his room and a corpse on the street. Brax jumped into his clothes, strapped on his iron, snatched up the bottle, and was gone. He was in the street and on the run by the time the crowd guessed where the body had come from. He spied a likely looking beast, a

gray mare with the makings of a strong desert rider. He was
no horsethief but a man does what he must. He flung himself
onto her back, kicked her hard with his bootheels, and
screamed in her ear. She thundered down the street. They
passed the mud huts on the edge of town, raising enough dust
to hide a locomotive, and horse and man were soon swallowed by the vast desert.

They covered five miles before Brax threw a glance over
his shoulder and realized no riders were in pursuit. He eased
up on the gray and brought her to a trot. A man who disap-
pears into the desert leaving a whore and a gunfighter dead
doesn't automatically draw a posse. That the man was a
gunfighter was beyond question. A glance at the well-used
crossdraw holster told Brax that. The narrow-brimmed hat
and kidskin duster pointed to higher country and a cooler
climate. Two things bothered him: he'd never seen the man
before, and he didn't know who wanted him dead. Brax
wasn't going to worry about the why. If he knew the who he
would know the why.

He sought a destination, and considered fording the river
into California. Sixty miles to the west lay El Centro. A poor
choice. They would remember Brax in El Centro. He once
spent three nights in jail there on a trumped-up drunk and
disorderly charge. When the sheriff came to let him out Brax
slugged him, took the gun and the tin star, then marched him
into the cell he had just vacated. In the corner stood the toilet
pail. Brax had pleaded in vain to have it emptied. Even after
five years they would remember Brax in El Centro. He
dragged that tinhorn lawman across the floor and forced his
bloated face into the rank, overflowing bucket. He had a
drink next door and caught the next stage out while the man
lay retching and gagging on the floor of the cell.

He turned east. The sun was peaking over the ragged crest
of the Gilas. As it cleared the mountains he sensed it was the
kind of day that would send the mercury over a hundred by
ten. This land belonged to that fireball. If hell was in the sky
this was purgatory on earth. To the west lay the Sand Hills, as

brutal a place for man and horse as ever there was, any time of year. To the north, the murderous Chocolate Mountains and the Trigo range, barren, forbidding knife blades thrusting a thousand feet from the desert floor. In any direction seeps were few and far apart. Only scraggly creosote dotted the playas, where each plant surrounds itself with a lifeless circle of earth.

Brax walked his tired mount up a lone hill where a fifty-mile view waited in any direction. A stray wind whipped up a feverish dust devil that whirled and twisted over the sand and rocks. Brax turned to the right, then to the east, then to the right again. He was sure now no one had followed him. In a town like Yuma folks weren't eager to step into private quarrels. Brax pivoted to face west again and stopped short.

The dust devil was still there and it didn't meander across the flats in the usual way. It was moving in a straight line, due east and right at him. With it came certain knowledge this was no trick of the wind. Another minute and Brax could see the rider clearly. One man on horseback, hell-bent and heading his way. The terrain offered Brax little cover. He was on a lone pyramid of rock in the center of a wide, empty valley.

The rider was a lean, dark man, an expert horseman who hugged the neck of his wiry stallion. Soon he would be in rifle range. Brax carried only a handgun, and it wasn't his style to shoot a man down from ambush. So he waited.

But not for long. The horseman jerked his mount to a halt and leaped out of the saddle, dropped to one knee on the run and raised his rifle to his shoulder. Brax scurried for cover and the bullet screamed into the rocks where his head had been a moment before.

It would have been easy, four years ago, to take a firm grip on the reins and calm the frightened mare, but now Brax yanked on the bit as he tried to lead her down the slope of the hill. When they reached a ledge where the land tilted less Brax got into the saddle and the mare began to slide, sending a shower of rocks down before them. Brax's hold on the reins became a series of hesitant jerks; the horse lost footing and panicked. It reared back and almost threw him. Another shot whizzed by his ear. The rifleman had circled around and was getting closer by the second.

They hit solid ground with a thud that nearly jarred him out of the saddle. Brax did not look back. He leaned into her and they took off at a dead run across the hard-packed flats of the Yuma Desert.

# Two

Froth trailed from the horse's bit. Vicente's Spanish roan pounded across the playa after the dustcloud that marked his quarry. They were exhausted. He knew he was pushing the horse to the limits now and cursed his hasty aim. He resolved not to miss again.

The relentless sun climbed, shadows vanished. The desert was a sweep of dazzling white light. Vicente was gaining, one more sprint might do it. He rowled the roan's flanks, asking for that last burst of power and getting it. The horse couldn't take much more of this. Vicente pulled the Winchester repeater out of the scabbard and strained his wiry leg muscles for balance. He raised the rifle to his shoulder. If he could get the rider in the sights for a moment, he would have him—picked off on the run.

Heedless of the rough terrain the faithful mount plunged ahead. The reins trailed from the pommel, slapping the saddle as Vicente drew a bead. Abruptly the land fell away into a wide dry riverbed, and the target was jarred from his sights. He swore and aimed again. The roan's forefoot went down into a hole scooped by running water. Vicente took a shallow breath. The horse's rear hoof came down, but the foreleg never came up. In the instant Vicente squeezed the trigger the stallion went down, at a full run. It tumbled head over heels and the rider was thrown twenty feet in the air.

He thudded into soft sand, the wind hammered out of him. He shook his head to clear the stars that danced before his eyes. The roan lay still, its eyes glazed over. Its shallow breath rattled and blood trickled from its nostrils. Vicente retrieved his rifle and put a bullet through its head.

He watched until his prey was lost to the glare and the dust, then undid the cinch and hoisted his saddle over his shoulder. Best to hide it, turkey vultures scrapping over the carcass might attract a passerby. He carried the saddle to a wetter slope that was blessed with paloverde and hid it among the trees. Winchester in hand and waterbag over his shoulder, Vicente Alvarez started walking.

It was twenty miles back to town. Already the heat played tricks with the light, tossing shimmering mountains on the horizon, but the young desert rat paced himself well and made good time. Before sundown he reached the outskirts of Yuma where the muddy Colorado separated the United States from one of its territories.

The shortest way to supplies and another horse was through the cemetery. Where Vicente walked no trees shaded the graves. This side was boot hill, where the poor, the unknown, and Indians and Mexicans were dumped into graves just deep enough to cheat the buzzards. He was looking for a freshly-turned mound of earth. On the respectable side of the graveyard, where cottonwoods and sycamores flourished, a funeral procession was wending up the hill. He paused to watch it. Fancy wagons and well-dressed mourners meant that a man of means was being laid to rest. Vicente kept walking, among simple headstones that bore Spanish names. Then he saw it. The new grave.

Some kind soul had placed a cross there, and had hung upon it a broken wooden rosary. Vicente took off his cotton sombrero, his only shade tree, baring his glossy black locks

to the late sun. He kneeled and held the rosary in his hands as
he prayed. When he finished he pulled the knife from the
crusty sheath under his shirt.

"Vaya con Dios, pequeña palama." And he carved one
word in the cross: ROSA.

At the livery he bought a lively five-year-old. Maybe he
could have picked up a cheaper mount by haggling with one
of the farmers on the outskirts of town but there was no time
for that. Anyway he couldn't turn this animal down. It was a
lucky horse. Another roan stallion.

He hitched it to the rail in front of Jon Perkins's supply
store and walked in. Perkins was bagging groceries. The
fleshy store-keeper moved with a slowness born of years in
the hot country. He paused to mop his dripping brow. His
customer, a dour-faced matron, was scolding a small boy for
some misdeed. Vicente glanced at the woman's floor-
sweeping skirt and the high-buttoned longsleeved blouse,
thought of the bustle and the petticoats, and wondered for the
thousandth time how women could stand those clothes in this
weather. To the obvious relief of the boy the woman turned to
the merchant and started small-talking.

Vicente needed food, ammunition, and a spare water bag.
It might be a long trip. He stood and waited, politely, while
the man he hunted rode towards Montana.

"Excuse me, Señor, Señora . . . I am in need of supplies,
and in some haste."

"Young man!" the woman snapped with a ferocity that
took him aback. "Don't you know it ain't polite to interrupt a
body when she's conversin'?"

"I meant no disrespect, but I must. . ."

Before Vicente could close his mouth she had turned back
to the clerk and was chattering again. This esteem in which
Vicente held women could be a drawback when it came to
serious business, but he resolved to keep his calm. If he could
run down Mescaleros and Yaquis, he could surely track any
gringo. He watched the boy wander over to the candy barrel,
fill his pockets to overflowing, and innocently reappear at the

woman's side by the time she was ready. They strolled out and Vicente barked his order, but it didn't hurry Perkins one bit.

He had everything secured to the makeshift saddle and was ready to mount up when his eye was snagged by the cantina cross the street. A momentary respite, a drink. To her. And a bottle, maybe, for the long trail. He never sampled that bottle last night, it was lost. Forgotten when he followed the men upstairs and they found her. He had acted, and let the heat of the chase crowd out his feelings. Then what was this he felt now? Anger he knew well . . . but grief?

It would take but moments. The gringo couldn't cover much ground in a day but Vicente, wise to the ways of the desert, would. One tequila for Rosa, and ride the lucky horse like the wind.

The saloon was a thick-walled mud cube with a skillfully thatched roof of ocotillo sticks and palm fronds. Short-lived twilight trickled through small square window holes in the adobe. The countertop stretched the twelve-foot width of the back wall. No one stood at the bar and only one of the three tables was in use. Four men ringed a reeking clutter of spilled tobacco and half empty bottles.

"Tequila," Vicente said to the bored man polishing the bar.

"Lookee there, Jimbo," the voice came from the table. "A visitor from the lovely land to the south." It was a thick bray, and it was meant to rankle. Vicente ignored it, paid, and drained his glass. The tequila was bad. It tasted like coal oil and burned like liniment.

"Hey, Pancho, you a stranger here?" Another voice, as cruel as the first. Vicente turned and headed for the door. There would be no bottle for this trip.

"I seen that face before." The biggest one spoke. This man had a face like a bloodhound. Loose folds of skin passed for features. "Last night, over at the Black Bull. He was there just before the shootin' upstairs."

They were hired hands or farmers, not gunslingers, tough,

angry men, like many Americans Vicente had known. Vicente smiled an engaging smile. He didn't want to be delayed by these louts.

"Señors," he said cheerfully, "I go now, and wish you well."

"Hold it, Greaseball!" The bloodhound lurched to his feet, swaying, and blocked the door. "I seen you twice. Just a little while ago, at Old Man Garvin's burial. You was walkin' 'round the graveyard."

"Sure, Jim, he was up in the Mex graveyard, by the new grave."

"The new grave?" He knitted his brow and the skin bunched up in his forehead like a mountain range. "Musta been the whore's grave."

Vicente slapped him, hard with an open palm, the way a man strikes a woman. The fleshy mouth jerked open like a trapdoor. The others watched a stinging welt appear on his cheek.

With a roar the big man seized a bottle by the neck and smashed it on the edge of the table. Vicente went fast for his gun but not fast enough. His hand stopped in mid-reach, caught in the vice-like grip of the burly saloonkeeper. The barman reached across him with his free hand and yanked the gun from its holster, then clamped a bearhug around the smaller man that nearly cracked his ribcage.

"Now, Greaseball . . ." Vicente watched the flaps of skin part into the widest grin he'd ever seen. The man's face was lost; Vicente found himself staring at the rotten tobacco-stained teeth that lined his maw. The beast waved the jagged end of the bottle. "Tell us about her!"

"Tell us what she did for a living!" Another rose unsteadily to his feet. "And how she loved it!" he jeered.

"How much she charge? How much she charge for a suck?"

"Speak up, Mex." He jabbed with the bottle. "Or wear these for eyeglasses!"

Vicente brought his legs together and kicked as hard as he

could. He caught his tormentor in the groin and the brute doubled over in agony. A fist slammed into Vicente's face and he felt himself blacking out. The bartender loosed his grip and he slid to the floor.

Vicente had to beat back the darkness that was slipping over him. In his mind's eye he saw himself kicked to death as he lay in the dirt. The men thought he was gone, but he roused, and then he was on his feet and the steel of his knife was flashing. There was the sound of ripping cloth and the bartender screamed. Blood welled from the slice in his forearm. Vicente scooped up his gun and the room froze. "I kill the first man who moves!"

He pictured a bull's-eye in the center of the big one's forehead and aimed straight for it, gestured with the muzzle and they huddled in the center of the room.

"Now hold on there son, we didn't mean no harm. . ." Vicente could smell the stink of the man's fear.

"Sure, take it easy," the speaker took a step forward. "We was just funnin' ya. . ."

Vicente cocked the gun pointedly. "Another step and you die," he said coolly. He backed out the door, still holding the sixshooter rock steady as he climbed onto the roan.

"Bastardos!" he spat. He jabbed the horse with his spurs and was gone.


The jackrabbit was stringy and tough, but mesquite coals made almost anything taste good. The dry air couldn't hang on to the late summer heat and the night was taking a turn towards the pleasant. By day the land seemed to lie dead under the unforgiving sun, but in the evening it came to life. Brax liked to imagine the teeming, hidden desert population. Cicadas whirred and wrens chattered, but above everything he could hear the coyote choir. He figured a hundred of the wily dogs prowled these hills. And over there in the folded uplands javelina nosed about hidden, slime-covered water holes, shoving their pig-like snouts into forbidding clumps of prickly pear and gobbling the cactus, spines and all.

Yes, it was sweet to be out here in the open wasteland, soaking up the sounds and the smells and the starlight. He'd forgotten how awesome the Arizona sky could be. Especially when not seen through barred windows or framed by eighteen-foot adobe walls. But the beauty of the night couldn't banish the nagging memory of the lone hunter of this morning. He'd vanished as suddenly as he appeared, and Brax was sure he hadn't simply given up and gone home for a cool drink.

Brax climbed the nearest hill and scanned the gently-sloping alluvial planes. These were the "bajadas," where storms washed down pieces of the mountain and spread them in vast fans of rock and sand. Shrubs and cactus, greedy for runoff water, soon greened the bajadas from valley floor to hilltop. In the moonlight the shadows of tree-sized cholla and giant saguaro formed a map-like network against the far hills.

He recalled the first time he'd seen the mighty saguaro cactus. It was near Tucson, where they grew so thick you could call them forests. Brax had seen thousands, and like men, each was different. On long rides he would play games with them in his mind, like finding fish and camels in the clouds. Here in lower, drier country the big cacti hardly put a dent in the emptiness, and he relished the sight of so much space after being penned like an animal for so long. But now that the time he had longed for in the closeness of his cell was here he didn't know what to do next.

Again he played with the notion of going to the coast, but no one in his right mind crossed southeast California this time of year without a damn good reason. He supposed he'd drift north, maybe climb the Mogollan where the heat wasn't so brutal. If he was smart he'd be done with the Territory altogether. Arizona was bad luck to Brax.

Yet the sweetness of being free in this vast harsh land almost overwhelmed him. He longed to give in to a flash of true joy, celebrate the sheer pleasure of being alive and in control of his life again. Suddenly he wanted to shout, jump, and run around like a little kid again, laugh out loud in the wind. Then he saw the rider.

This time he saw it for what it was the moment his eyes caught movement in the valley below. This horseman was raising no dust, his movements were slow and full of purpose. Now and again the tracker stopped to scan the hills. He was looking for a campfire. Brax decided to give him one.

He had to move swiftly. He built the fire of mesquite wood and cholla skeletons, then tethered his mare where she could be seen from below. As a final touch he laid his bedroll over rocks near the campfire. Brax didn't intend to let anyone close enough to see no man lay under it. He made his way down the hill and around to the side that would seem safest to a man intent on surprising the camp and ducked behind a boulder to wait.

He watched the tracker lead his horse to a wash and conceal it with great care behind a massive ironwood tree. Crouching low and cradling his rifle in his arms, the man sprinted towards the false camp. He ran a zig-zag pattern, ducking behind rocks every twenty yards or so as he worked his way up the hill. The closer he got the more time he spent hidden, listening, watching for any movement above. This character meant business.

He was a slender, light-stepping man, sure-footed as a puma and silent as an Apache. He was not an Indian, if one could judge by the cut of his clothes or the style of riding. He was dark-skinned, a halfbreed, maybe, and young. When he achieved rifle range he didn't train his weapon but kept coming. He meant to be sure of his shot, or confront his quarry face-to-face.

Brax held his breath. His gun hand was twitching. He uncurled his trigger finger and flexed it. Soon his legs would ache; he had been crouching for many minutes and they were stiff. The man glided past. Brax could see the brocade on the band on his sombrero, the hat tied back over his shoulders to make for a smaller target. Brax had seen enough.

"Tip one more toe and I'll bring you down, boy."

Vicente froze in his tracks.

# Three

"Now drop the rifle and bring your hands together. Over your head, high as you can reach. And stand still! Don't blink, don't breathe, don't sweat." Brax came up from behind and jerked Vicente's pistol from its holster. "All right, let's have a look at you."

Dark eyes blazed from finely sculpted mestizo features. Brax took him to be about twenty. He wasn't a big man but he was muscular. And well-equipped for desert travel. A professional tracker?

"Who hired you to tail me?"

Vicente looked past the gun to the man and stared a hole in his thoughts. So this weary-looking cowboy was the killer. It was a warm face, not what he had expected. But of course such men are like anyone else. Except they kill women.

"I wish to unclasp my hands, Señor."

"Soon as I get your pigsticker, amigo." Brax pulled the knife from the sheath and patted him down in search of another one or a derringer. "All right, get those boots off."

"Señor?"

"I won't say it again."

Brax tossed the boots into the bushes behind him. "Man thinks twice about running through cholla barefoot," he muttered.

The boy began to cross himself. "Madre de Dios. . ."

"What are you doing? Get those paws up, goddamn it!"

Vicente glared at him. "I am unarmed. Shall I strip?"

"No."

"Then I make peace with my God."

"Peace with your God?"

"I don't ask you to send for a priest," he said crossly.

"Sit down! Over there. Don't be giving me a reason to pull the trigger. 'Cause I sure as hell don't need much of one. I'm not forgetting you took a shot at me back there." Vicente dropped to the ground on crossed legs, Indian-style. Brax found a natural chair in the rocks a few feet away and settled in. "It *was* you back there, right?" Vicente nodded. "Good," said Brax. "Means there's not two wild-eyed desert rats after my hide. Now you didn't answer me. Who sent you?"

"I work for no man!" Vincente spat. "And if you do not kill me I will follow you again. And again. Until I kill you."

Brax didn't need to ponder it. "I think you might at that. You better get those mitts back up. Plenty of time for mumblin' and crossin' yourself later." The young man sat rock still. Brax found his stare unnerving. "Why?" he asked after the blazing eyes forced him to look away. "Why do you want to kill me?"

"Why? You ask *why?*"

Brax shrugged. "Reasonable, isn't it? 'Pears a number of people have quarrel with me. Maybe you can help sort it out."

"Señor," Vicente spoke softly. "Are you a liar, or merely a fool?"

"Probably a bit of both," Brax snapped. "Now answer me and be quick about it!" He cocked the Colt and straightened his shooting arm, bringing the muzzle up, a foot away from Vicente's forehead. "Buzzards got to eat too, kid," he reminded him.

"Rosa," Vicente said.

"Rosa?" Brax fished for the connection. "Oh, Rosa. The girl." He shook his head. "I didn't kill her."

"No? Who then?"

Brax lowered the pistol. "The man who killed her is dead."

Vicente looked doubtful. "The man on the boardwalk?"

"That's the one."

"The dead man, outside?"

Brax nodded. Vicente thought on it. "It may be as you say. But it is no matter."

"I don't get it, kid. Was she something special to you?"

"Perhaps *you* would like to answer a question. We shall see what a clever liar you are."

"Maybe. What is it?"

"What was she doing in your room, Señor?"

"In *my* room?" Brax knitted his brow. "Oh hell! She was the maid, come to clean up. Innocent bystander."

Vicente took a deep, patient breath. "I am young, Señor, but I am no idiot. Do chambermaids in this country work naked?"

"Uh . . ." Brax had forgotten.

"Perhaps you did not shoot her," Vicente conceded. "I can never know that. But you have taken her honor, and it must be avenged."

"*Taken her honor?*" spluttered Brax. "Now listen, kid," he managed when he recovered. "You're no idiot, like you said. I can see that, way you tracked me and all. So you know things aren't always as they seem, right kid?"

"Please, Señor. Do not address me as 'keed.' "

"What then?"

"Vicente Alvarez."

"My name's Brax. She your sister? What was she to you?"

"*What was she doing in your room naked,* Señor?"

"Now look here, who's holding the gun on who?" But Vicente just glowered at him.

"O.K., kid, here it is. I didn't know her. She did it for pay. That's the way it was."

Somewhere a single coyote barked. A moment later the desert answered with a hundred yips.

"You lie!" He had springs in his legs. He was on his feet and coming fast.

"Stay put, damn it!" Brax shouted as he raised the Colt again. Vicente sat.

He stared into the dust. "You lie," he repeated.

"No," said Brax. How many minutes passed? Three? Ten?

Vicente broke the silence. "You have no reason to lie?" he said at last and raised his eyes.

"No," Brax said. "I have no reason to lie. Would have killed you already if I did." Again the silence threatened to close in on them. Vicente pursed his lips, inclined his head in what might have passed for a nod. Brax stumbled on. "She saved my life. Took a bullet meant for me." Somehow it wasn't enough. "She warned me. I owe her my life."

"It . . . it makes sense now," Vicente spoke in a flat, even tone. "El *correo,* never a letter for me. Only money, each month money for her dear, sweet madre." His eyes sought Brax's. "Señora Felix must never know," he said gravely.

"Oh no," said Brax. "Señora Felix will never know." He fumbled for his matches, was surprised to see he was still pointing the gun at him. He holstered it and got a hold on his pouch and papers. Reluctant to take his eyes off the younger man, he botched the first smoke and had to roll another. But Vicente wasn't moving. His eyes were on the ground again.

Vicente wasn't looking at the pale gray-green clump of hedgehog cactus between his feet and his mind wasn't on Brax. For he was no longer in the here and now of the Arizona wasteland on this balmy night. He was back in his home state of Chihuahua and the time was just over a year ago. . . .

The sun is high overhead, so high that he casts almost no shadow as he labors over the broken axle. The old wooden-wheeled *carreta* is loaded with vegetables from the mission garden. He was bound for the city until the axle splintered. It froze the big wobbling wheel in its track.

Vicente straightens, wipes his brow, and squints down the road where a tiny black speck shimmers, swimming in the waves of super-heated air that rise from the barren ground. It moves so slowly it seems to grow no larger as the sweltering minutes tick by. And anyway the sweat is cascading off Vicente's forehead and flowing into his eyes. It's making a blur of everything. He removes his work sombrero and shakes it. Perspiration rains onto the ground and soaks into the dust. Again he wipes his brow and his eyes and stoops to his task.

It is only with a mighty effort that he can wrest that wheel off. The cart shifts on the stones that are propping it up but his makeshift jack holds. He can see now how badly the axle is cracked. He binds it with maguey rope. Not much of a repair but he doesn't have far to go. A flat rock will do as a hammer. He spies one in the sand, lays his hand on it and gasps out loud. The sun has been beating on the damn thing for hours, the stone is shockingly hot. He unslings his waterbag and wets the stone down, an unthinkable use of water if he weren't so close to town. Meanwhile the speck down the road has made some progress. Vicente doesn't take much notice but it is near enough to be recognized. It's a wagon with two people in the seat behind four mules. Vicente pulls on the flat rock and it comes free with a sucking noise. Centipedes quickly uncoil and scuttle in all directions, ugly red and black things half a foot long, running for their lives from a midday sun that threatens to sear them like tortillas thrown on mesquite coals. "Hola!" calls the driver of the wagon.

Vicente has the wheel poised over the damaged axle but the axle has swelled more than he thought and of course it is bone dry. If Vicente can pound the wheel back on it may grudgingly grant the two thousand turns or so needed to reach the city. More likely it will groan and grind and splinter even more. In the arid heat it might even spark and burn. Vicente is contemplating whittling the axle down when the driver of the wagon appears beside him.

He is elderly but stands erect and carries himself with the bearing of a much younger man. His delicate Castilian features are complemented by proud straight silver hair, but his skin is as dark as Vicente's. Vicente looks up at him and remembers his manners. As he straightens to greet the old gentleman his eyes are captured by *her*.

She's beautiful and young, a year or two younger than Vicente. A fawn-like thing, tawny, smooth and slender and everything's the right size and in the right place. Vicente stares—at the tiny beads of sweat that coat her full upper lip, at her mouth poised between a smile and a pout. Her features are more sensuous than delicate, with high cheekbones and fleshy chin. Her face is small and round and nearly copper-colored. She has a small nose, just a little flat, and her forehead is low. And the eyes—they're the huge full-of-hope eyes of a tabby kitten. They are a deep chocolate brown.

An airy shawl, white under the coating of dust, keeps the sun off her shoulders. A scarf of the same insubstantial material covers her ink-black, bunched-up, half-breed hair. More sweat, large drops of it, dapple her arms, which are browner than her face. Vicente's eyes follow her slim arms to the hands. There is no ring. His gaze flashes back to those eyes. They meet his briefly and a trace of a smile twitches her lips.

"I said I have grease here, young man."

The old fellow has stooped to examine Vicente's cart. Vicente realizes he has not heard. He recovers somewhat clumsily and introduces himself with a bow. The man points with a slender, leather-like hand that is bedizened with four or five silver and turquoise rings. "Ah, but this will not take you to the next arroyo," he is saying. "In a dozen turns it will split as a log under the woodsman's awl. Are you bound for the city? We have room for you and your small load." He draws his lips back in a wide smile and a mouthful of gold flashes. He nods his head towards the produce in the bed of Vicente's cart. "But I think in town you will have to trade those for some proper wagon tools, no?"

Her name was Rosa Maria Felix; her father's, Pedro. Vicente hitched his burro behind and rode on the seat, between them. They talked of the city market, and vegetables, and the bad dry year—bad even for Chihuahua, for the winter rains hadn't come that year. Soon Vicente found himself talking about his village, not far from theirs, and the mission, and Brother Salcido's worthy scholarly pursuits. "I too can read and write," he blurted with an uncharacteristic lack of modesty which he instantly regretted.

"And so can Rosa!" Señor Felix proclaimed with obvious pride. "She is the best student in the village!"

"Poppa, you shame me!"

"Señor!" Vicente croaked and laid a hand on the old man's arm. "Look!" He pointed to the far ridge. Señor Felix squinted into the sun to make out a half a dozen mounted figures silhouetted on the mesa, immobile as the rocks upon which they stood. Vicente already had his pistol out of his waistband. The old man just shrugged. "The Apache grows bolder," Vicente said, trying to keep the quiver out of his voice. "I have never known him so near the city. Doesn't it frighten you?"

"Bah!" he spat. "The Apache, he feasts off the gringo. But here. . . ." He patted his old but spotless rolling-block rifle. "Here he will get his just dessert!" As if to lend truth to his words, the warriors turned their mounts and disappeared into the cliffs.

In the city center Vicente thanked his benefactors and asked if he might be so bold as to call upon them soon.

As has been the way of Spanish families from time immemorial, *los novios* were never permitted to be alone together. And as has been the way of sweethearts for just as long, Vicente and Rosa sidestepped the rules as often as possible. The upcoming fandango in Rosa's village was eagerly awaited for just this reason. Sometimes the easiest place to be alone is in a crowd. And if you do manage to get away, you're less likely to be missed when the wine flows and the night rings with music and laughter.

Their first fiesta together was in the fall when the shepherds and the vaqueros moved their charges from the highlands down into the warmer valleys for the winter. Though he did not work with cattle Vicente joined the procession of *los charros*, for his horsemanship was the equal of most of them. Proudly he sat upon his small brown mare, her Arabian bloodline showing in every prancing step. Like the others he wore leather pantaloons embossed with silver buttons and jingling chains, a short jacket of the finest cowhide, and his best sombrero with its braids of silver and gold. The clothes represented several months' wages and a half-serious dressing-down from his tolerant Franciscan mentor but it was well worth it.

And Rosa? In a full skirt, blood-red and spangled with blue and green and yellow; a low-cut, snow-white blouse with silk embroidery and a hundred gaily colored hand-sewn beads; and a rebozo of the brightest blue, so fine it could be drawn through a wedding ring, folded smoothly about her waist. Vicente and Rosa danced the *jarabe,* a dance brought to their desert villages years ago by travelers from the far south. At the end of the dance, when she danced on the brim of his hat and swooped it up off the floor he swung his leg over her with perfect timing and they bowed to great applause.

It should have been a marvelous evening. Though Vicente drank only a little wine that night he was drunk—drunk with that clear-headed intoxication that comes from just the right amount of good drink at the right time, and from being in love. That night Vicente's world was sharp and bright and crystal-clear. The stars blazed white in the inky black of the sky, white adobe was the color of mountain snow, and the dust was the shiny red of a wet rooster's plumage.

But others that night were not so charmed. Where tequila and *cerveza* flow in quantity tempers may wear thin as the

night wears on. All evening a great muscle-bound laborer had
been harassing a slightly-built herder who Vicente knew and
liked. The bully would cut in on the shepherd's dances,
mouthing snide comments and thinly-veiled threats. The
smaller man shrugged it off until the big one crowded his
woman.

It was getting late. Vicente and Rosa saw their chance to
steal away for a few precious moments alone. They rounded a
corner just off the plaza and almost collided with the two
battling men. It was obvious this was no contest. The larger
man was fast as well as strong. He toyed with the herder,
spinning him around and slapping him about at will. But
there was no mirth in this sport. At any moment he might pick
the little man off his feet and dash his brains out against the
wall.

Though Rosa pulled at him, urging him away, Vicente
couldn't leave. Should he intervene? He might spare the
shepherd serious injury, possibly his life. But he'd surely
make an enemy of him, for the rescued man would rightly
feel his honor was compromised. Vicente had made his
reluctant decision and was ready to turn and follow her when
to their utter astonishment a blade flashed and the bully
staggered back, gasping horribly. He died even as he tried to
stuff the flowing entrails back into his ripped belly.

Rosa was shattered. It was the first time death had come
before her eyes. Vicente did his best to comfort her but she
was inconsolable for days. Vicente had seen a few men die
but it was always neat and clean, from a far-off and imper-
sonal bullet. There was a lesson here, he realized as he
brooded over the spoiled evening. He had witnessed the
power of a skillfully wielded knife in the hands of a much
smaller man. A short time later he would find the knife-
fighter and expand their fledgling friendship. For a number of
weeks Vicente spent his leisure time at the sheep camp.
While the man worked with his knives, honed them, made
sheathes and practiced feinting and throwing, Vicente
watched, listened, imitated, and learned.

Only five months had passed since that fiesta when Vicente and Rosa stood over the coffin and looked upon the
rouged, wax-like face of her father. Señor Felix was found
face-down in a filthy irrigation ditch shortly after two halfbreed strangers had left the village. The old rifle, the one he
was so proud of, was gone. It was the weapon that had fired
the bullets that killed him. His body had been stripped. The
gold in his mouth was gone and the fingers that wore the
silver rings had been hacked off. At least the undertaker did a
fair job and his wife and daughters were spared the knowledge of this outrage.

A brutal and pointless death. During the wake, as he sat
drinking and playing cards with the male mourners Vicente
sized up potential avengers to the atrocity. The prospects
were dismal. Most were elderly men lacking the vigor of their
murdered relative. The rest were distant relations content to
leave the sorry matter in the hands of the local police.

Like bad mescal Vicente's anger soured his insides, a
festering sickness that only dogged resolution could cure. It
may have been the hollow agonized look that clouded Rosa's
lovely eyes. Or the heart-rending sight of little Carlotta, too
young to understand, standing by the gaily-painted coffin
blithely sucking on one of the sugar-candy skulls the children
loved so. She would never appreciate her grandfather's kindness, nor reap the benefits of his intuitive understanding of
life. Surely tragedy stalked this family—the little one's
father, Rosa's brother and the dead man's only son—had also
died violently and needlessly, an innocent bystander cut
down by feudists in a bordertown cantina.

For Vicente an hour of sport-shooting in the convento
garden was now no longer enough. In the small hours of the
night he would steal away into the dark and empty badlands
where none could see or hear. By dawn tin and glass targets
littered the desert and rifle and handgun were hot from use.
On some nights he set up scarecrows and shredded them with
his knives, feinting, jabbing and throwing until his arms were
dead with fatigue. Each morning he cleaned and oiled his

weapons before sneaking to the mission just in time for breakfast.

In the evenings he tried to comfort his love. They were alone often now, but Vicente could not duck from the shadow of Brother Salcido and his mission teachings.

"Haceme amor, Vicente. . ."

No, he told her, no. We must wait, we must be patient. When your mother no longer mourns him we will be married.

And then one day Vicente heard of two renegades who boasted of yanking the gold from an old man's mouth, cutting the rings off his fingers and then shooting him with his own rifle. . . .

They had a full day's lead on him but their trail was a thing of beauty. They were big men who needed heavy horses and the tracks were deep. By sundown of the first day their sign grew even clearer. The droppings were still damp and Vicente felt the exhilaration of the hunter closing on his prey. But this prey did not stop for the night. They pushed on and were near the border by dawn.

That year summer came early to the desert grasslands of southeast Arizona. The bunchgrass shriveled although it had been put to the torch. Streams and springs slowed to a trickle or disappeared altogether. Worst of all, the ground baked into rock-hard pavement. He lost their tracks just north of the border until a synpathetic *paisano* steered him northwest.

The compatriot's story was soon confirmed, for the outlaws left a trail of slaughtered wildlife and fouled waterholes in their wake. Skirting the Chiricahuas, the mountain stronghold of the great Apache chief Cochise when he held Arizona at bay a generation before, they crossed the torrid Sulphur Springs Valley. These men were skilled riders and their mounts were strong. Vicente rode a light-boned mare with little experience in crossing wide stretches of waterless country. He had to push her harder than he wanted to. Once they were out of the open country he was able to dismount and walk her. At dusk in a nameless foothill canyon in the Dragoons the exhausted man and horse stumbled upon life-saving springs. Vicente was on his belly with his face in the water when he heard them.

He snatched his pistol from his waistband as he rolled to the safety of the rocks. It was a man's voice, and the unmistakable clop of shod hooves on rocky terrain. Vicente was propped on his elbows in good cover, pistol cocked and ready, just as he'd practiced. But now the voice was gone and only the sound of the horse remained, a weak and rapidly fading echo. Several minutes passed before he realized where the sounds had come from.

With little need for haste he stood and walked to the mare. She was calmly grazing on the relatively lush growth carpeting the area. He pulled his rifle from the saddle boot and checked the load and action before picketing the horse, kneeled at the spring again to fill his waterbag, then slung the waterbag over his shoulder in preparation for the climb. He looked over the ground he had to cover. Not too bad. A gentle slope about halfway up, then plenty of rocky handholds and footrests the rest of the way.

Here the mountains flowed into the plains in a series of roughly parallel ridges, like the spread fingers of an outstretched hand. Canyons lay between them. When Vicente gained the summit of the ridge he looked down into a canyon very much like the one he'd left. It was a long narrow U running north and south. He stood near the south end where an impassable verticle wall—the side of a mountain—prevented exit. About five hundred feet below him and a quarter of a mile further down the canyon a bold and merry campfire glowed. In the campsite, almost encircled by man-sized boulders, sat the two murderers.

For an intense hour Vicente sifted his information. For arms, he had to assume they carried at very least the stolen rifle. It was a single-shot breechloader, this he knew, and perhaps four seconds were needed to reload after firing. In that time Vicente's repeating rifle could kill them both. He also knew the old man's gun was one of the most accurate distance weapons in the world with half again the range of

Vicente's Winchester. And there were two of them to do the shooting. There was probably a lever-action repeater in that camp as well. Obviously Vicente had no advantage in firepower.

Scrupulously he studied the land, determined to make the most of every second of fading light. He tried to commit to memory each fold, gully, and boulder before night chased them away. The situation did not look good. Out of habit, it seemed, the bandits had chosen a well-protected site. Even worse, the hills that would place Vicente within firing range were barren and sloped gently, their vein-like gullies too narrow and shallow to hide a man. Only the north end of the canyon where it opened into the desert like the mouth of a river offered any hope of an ambush.

At least he was getting a handle on it. He could wait until they broke camp in the morning. Problem was, the north pass was not necessarily the obvious exit. North could be out of their way, or they might avoid a potential ambush site like this out of habit. In any case the hills which formed a good portion of the west wall of the canyon presented no serious obstacle to experienced riders like these. Now that the business had been simplified into how to insure they leave by the north pass, Vicente allowed himself the luxury of a little optimism.

And then the answer popped into his head. Simple inspiration, really. He visualized the project in its entirety and went to work on it at once. If he pulled it off, the murderers would think they were surrounded on three sides and under siege. Under those circumstances most men who traveled light would take their chances on the open desert, which lay to the north.

Vicente gathered the coarse brush first, then selected cliff vines of a uniform thickness from which to make his fuses. Four or five fires stretching in a line along both ridges ought to do the trick. Under the cloak of a moonless evening he picked his way first up one ridge then backtracked along the opposite ridge. Every hundred yards or so he built a small

brushpile over a handful of pistol cartridges and timed the trip
between each of these firesites. Well out of their line of sight,
he burned a length of the vine and timed that. It was a simple
matter to cut and place the fuses accordingly.

And he would start it all by opening up with his Winchester. The bullets would fall far short but there is something
very convincing in the sound of .44 caliber slugs screaming
off the rocks. He raised the rifle to his shoulder and squeezed
off four rapid-fire shots. He lit the fuse of the first fire,
sprinted to the second and lit that, then raced on to the third.
When he reached the last fire the explosions began. The
mountains reeled under the din of the gunfire. The echoes
pursued each other madly between the canyon walls; an
impossible cannonade. There was no time to admire the
work, he had to dash along the top of the hills above their
camp and past it to the deadly sheltered walls of the north
pass. He took up residence and waited.

And waited. Until the roar of his phantom army ceased.
Until a full ten minutes had passed and the moon peeked over
the cliffs. When it was fully up he climbed down into the false
daylight of the silent canyon and found the cleft that ran due
east, neat as you please, through the ridge, out of the mountains and out of his reach.

Only a scuff mark on the stone, a broken shrub, and most
convincing of all, the fact that this was the only possible
avenue of escape betrayed them. With the cunning of the
hunted they now took great pains to conceal their tracks.
Vicente covered many miles before he again picked up a clear
trail. Always they stayed a day, half a day, an hour ahead of
him, finding comfort and safety in boomtown hellholes and
hardscrabble Indian reservations. The season wore on—
hotter, drier, more dangerous by the day. And still they
eluded him. Finally they wandered up the valley of the Rio
Grande and east into the Tulorosa Basin, planning to ren-
dezvous with others of their kind in the tree-shaded heights
of the San Andres.

Their camp was on the very edge of the snow-colored

dunes that shift across the floor of the valley. Again it was a good campsite. It was hidden from curious eyes by jumbled rocks and thick growths of Mormon Tea but a well-meaning visitor from the mountains betrayed them. From his high perch in the foothills Vicente watched the visitor making his way, ant-like, across the dazzling sand in the heat of the day to warn his comrades of a dark and sullen young man. A young man who was asking about the two of them in Los Cruces and was certainly headed their way. Vicente waited until the messenger departed, then moved, even as the two killers were making their own plans to ambush their pursuer.

The first one set out to reconnoiter the west rim of the basin, checking for signs with a skill nearly equal to Vicente's. From his present position, Vicente could see him clearly. The second man, he assumed, would scour the southern and southeastern rims of the basin. Drawing upon all of his experience as a hunter and tracker Vicente began a slow and silent descent. Their decision to split their forces, he vowed, would be a fatal one.

Forty minutes later Vicente Alvarez, a young man in love, stood over a man staked out in the sun over the unyielding spikes of a vicious desert lilly, the Spanish Bayonet. He waited for the pain to wrest the man back to consciousness. When the diseased, yellow-tinged eyes sprang wide he stared straight into them. ''For the old man,'' he whispered. He stooped to check the gag over the helpless man's mouth and left him.

The other was not to be so easy. With great care Vicente entered the camp. He was intent on hiding any food, water, or weapons they had left behind. If Vicente didn't make it out of this valley no one would. And he almost didn't, because the camp wasn't empty.

The head popped up from behind a rock and a rifle thundered. But God and the hunted man's panic were on Vicente's side. The bullet flew past him and plowed into a dirt rise. Vicente dropped to one knee, raised the stock of his own long gun to his shoulder, and got off one quick shot.

What happened next passed in a few seconds but Vicente's mind was to snatch every detail. The first thing that occurred was the man's right eye vanished. In its place appeared a small but spreading red crater. While the echoes of the shots still sounded off the hillsides the man's rifle fell and clattered on the stones. His hands reached for his ruined face but they never made it. Instead his body toppled forward, passed through a thornbush, and sprawled over the rocks. There was no twitching; it lay perfectly still. Slowly out from under the face flowed a thin, dark rivulet. It dripped down the side of a stone scoured smooth by the wind and the water and pooled in the dust. The flow ceased and a brown stain formed on the rock as the blood dried in the arid breeze.

Vicente took a step forward, stopped, then walked through the space that separated them. He stood over the fresh corpse, seized the black hair and pulled the dead face off the ground.

A few minutes later he was crossing the dunes on his way back to his first victim, resolved to keep the image of Señor Felix in the forefront of his thoughts. He heard the whimpers of the dying man, reached the crest of a low dune and the grisly scene came into view. Señor Felix—a kindly, elderly, innocent man, sent to a cold grave in so appalling a manner—did not such a crime merit a death like this?

No! As God made heaven and earth, there would be no rasping croaks and jaundiced eyes to shatter his sleep! He stepped back five paces, then five more. He pulled his pistol, squinted into the sun and drew a bead on the man's head. It was only another can or bottle, like the hundreds riddled or shattered during his hours of shooting practice. Through a blur of tears Vicente fired.

When he looked upon his work he sank to his knees and retched. He spewed his meager breakfast over the sand and somehow it defiled the whiteness worse than blood. He covered it, the way a cat buries its excrement. He looked back only once, from a high notch in the hills. Far below the two black billowing shapes stood out against the brilliant white sand. The shapes were flocks of squabbling, hump-backed buzzards, already feasting while others wheeled and soared under the sun.

It took him a week to make his way back. The high sun of early summer left his face blistered and raw and his lips nearly black. The skin of his hands was so cracked and split it pained him for weeks. Behind were two good horses ridden to death and rotting in the wastelands. At last in the relative cool of the evening he stumbled up to the house of his beloved. Her joy at his safe return was unrestrained. Until he yanked the two stinking, gore-flecked scalps from his belt and threw them at her feet.

But *why?* It was a question he was to ask himself time and time again in the empty days and nights that followed—why this brutal and shocking gesture? Did he blame *her* for his first blood? Or was it some kind of punishment, retribution for her failure to be the virtuous and unspoiled creature of his unrealistic longings?

"Haceme amor, Vicente." Her words were a mocking litany. And Señora Felix never did seem to come out of mourning. And now Rosa would be away from home for days at a time, and the Señora didn't seem to know or care. Until one day Rosa told him of an aunt he'd never heard of who lived among the Norteamericanos, a seamstress and a milliner serving the people of the old Yuma Crossing and the town that had grown up there. Rosa would learn well from her, how to design fancy hats and embroider for the wealthy gringo ladies. Vicente must continue to study and work hard and save his pesos, soon they would be together again, she said, and the time would be right to be married, and Vicente was almost sure, for a time, that he believed her.

"No!" He shook his head from side to side roughly, almost violently.

"Smoke?"

The clump of hedgehog cactus at his feet came back into focus as the shaking subsided.

"I said do you want a smoke, kid?"

Lost like a man coming out of a deep sleep, he just stared

for a moment, then nodded his head. Brax tossed the Bull Durham. The pouch slipped from Vicente's fingers and he had to lean over to retrieve it. Brax saw the tears that had welled up in his eyes.

Hastily Vicente turned away. He deftly rolled a cigarette and fired it. "Gracias," he said. An acrid gray cloud plumed from his mouth and nose. He stood. "I will go now. And I will not trouble you again."

A man like Brax, who believed nothing of what he heard and little of what he saw, could count the people he trusted on the fingers of one hand. And even that might be stretching it. But there are times when one man sizes up another in a way that seems to run up against the known facts. Because this young greaser—who had just tried to kill him for the second time—appealed to something Brax was sure had been dead for a long time.

Twenty-odd years ago he had been as full of feelings and fire as Vicente. But any faith Brax had in the goodness of men and women had gone up in smoke, along with the gray rags the Confederate States of America had called a uniform. But for that goddamn war he might be raising crops and kids somewhere in northeast Texas. A son would be about the same age as this Vicente.

And if there had been any illusions slumbering under that sunburned hide of his, Brax was sure he'd dumped the last of them in the snake den on Prison Hill.

Brax jerked his head in the direction of the fire. "Let's go on up to camp." He stood and started walking. But for the sound of his boots crunching in the gravel all was quiet, then he heard the young Mexican scramble to his feet.

Vicente felt the need to explain. "We were engaged to be married. I rode from Chihuahua to surprise her. We . . . did not know one another long."

Brax pointed to the bushes. "Your boots, kid."

Vicente picked them up. "I guess we did not know each other at all."

"Come on." Brax had an urge to put his hand on the kid's shoulder. "I've got some java and half a bottle."

"Tequila?"

"Whisky. Good old-fashioned rotgut rye."

They sipped and smoked. Most of the time Vicente just stared into the fire and Brax let him be. The kid had opened up plenty for one night. The moon began its roll down the sky. Before long the pink-gray fingers of dawn would reach for it. There'd be little sleep this night. Brax allowed as how he'd sooner rest up through the hot part of the day anyway. Only Gila monsters, scorpions, and lunatic Mexicans—he glanced at his companion—were about in the heat of the day. And even lizards and bugs took to the shadows when the sun stood straight.

Moonlight turned to dawn and Brax started drifting. His eyelids dropped and images came to him in his half-slumber. Again the memories, flitting somewhere on the edge of his thoughts, threatening to turn into a full-scale nightmare. Yuma! He roused with a start. The kid had nudged him and was offering the bottle.

Just about empty and Brax was broke. No matter. Better to drink whisky now than later, the way liquor dried a man up. If his memory served him, the next step north held out a full day's ride. He looked at his companion, finally starting to nod in the half-light of false dawn. No doubt he'd be on his way this afternoon and Brax would be alone again. The way he liked it, really. Only this kid knew the desert and might come in handy. If Brax missed that step he'd have to backtrack all the way to the river.

"Lodgepole." Vicente broke into his thoughts.

"Kid," Brax was staring out into the desert. "I think I missed something. Or maybe you thought you told me something only you was dreaming it."

"When I got to Yuma, I carried many days' trail. I went to the hotel to freshen up."

"So?"

"So it was the hotel where . . . Rosa died."

"That's how you tailed me."

"Si. I was in the saloon downstairs. It was crowded. I had to fight my way to the bar to get a drink. There I stood next to three men. One man left. I saw this man a few minutes later. On the walk outside your room, with holes in him."

"You get a good look at the other two?"

"I have done better than that. I told you where they were going. They complained of the heat and were anxious to leave town, to return to Lodgepole."

"Huh."

"You know the place?"

"Gold town."

"Ghost town," Vicente corrected. "The gold, I hear it is played out."

"Played out. Like my old partner."

"Your old partner, Señor Brax?"

"The man who told me about Lodgepole. I couldn't travel at the time of the strike, so he went up to stake a claim."

"And did he find gold? Only a few found gold."

Brax shrugged. "Never did hear. I expect he's drifted away or got himself killed. Town's shut down, eh?"

"No more mining. A few ranches in the area, but the town? It is said only thieves live there." It was a familiar story. The high-living boom town lingers on after its legs have been shot out from under it. "In any event, we shall see for ourselves what sort of place this Lodgepole is, no?"

Brax turned away. He could barely be heard. "I just want to be left alone."

"You . . . you will not follow them?" Vicente couldn't believe his ears.

"Look, the guy mistook me for someone. Or . . . maybe he was sweet on Rosa; I ain't tryin' to rub it in, but could be, right?"

Vicente shook his head. "No, Señor. I distinctly heard one man say the word 'Braxton.' That is some coincidence, eh? That is your name, no? You think they will forget you? I think not. Señor, someone wants you dead."

"Lots of folks want me dead." Brax raised the bottle and drained the last of the whisky.

"So what does one do, spend his life running, like the jack-rabbit from el coyote?"

"I've had trouble aplenty for a goddamn lifetime."

"There is no question here, Señor," he said firmly. "And I must avenge Rosa's death. I owe her that much."

"You owe her nothing!"

A stab of hurt came and went. He spoke with conviction. "Then I owe *you*, Señor Brax."

"Shit, it's getting too hot to argue." 'Specially with a Mex kid with lava in his veins instead of blood. And heart instead of sense. "Do what you like," he spat, "I'm gettin' some sleep." He spread his bedroll under a rock overhang and lay down. "Time sun gets in here, I'll be ready to move. Don't know where but I'm sure as hell not staying here."

Vicente knew full well where they were going. "Señor Brax."

"What?" grumped Brax from his bed.

"I'm glad I missed."

"So am I," Brax admitted, and rolled over and slept.

# Four

Harv Jordan could see most of Lodgepole from the windows of his suite above the saloon. A few years ago no town blighted the forested tableland. Until word got out the riverbed was coated with dreams, soft flakes of high-grade golden dreams. Placers only, but surely it could be found in nuggets—or tons—if one had the strength and patience to knock down the mountain.

Like so many times in so many places in the West a city sprouted overnight. But a year later the truth was known. Lodgepole was the flower that blooms before the last killing frost. This was not another Sutter's Mill or Nevada Comstock, and there was no "mother lode."

First the bank closed, then the sheriff's office. Now only the sporting crowd remained to postpone the town's inevitable fate. Local ranchers and homesteaders avoided the place; to them it was worth an extra day's ride to the Mormon settlements. Lodgepole was on no circuit-riding lawman's agenda, and the men who stayed had no regrets. Losers, drifters, and wanted men schemed their lives away trading cash, drinks, and lies over Harv Jordan's gaming tables.

Jordan turned off the glare of the sun and the ugliness of the town with a yank of his curtains, drew back the folding jalousie doors of his walk-in closet and began his morning ritual. Today he passed over the blue cut-away waistcoat of English worsted in favor of a black four-button squarecut. He left the sharply creased matching trousers on the rack and selected a pair of black and gray pinstripes. He would wear a brocaded vest of French silk over a pleated white shirt with starched collar and large black square knot tie and top it off with his twenty-two-carat gold watch and fob. For the shoes, Jordan favored llama-skin ankle-highs.

Jordan knew that an expensive getup commands respect, but there was more to it than that. He genuinely loved the look and feel of fine clothes. Outfitting his six-foot four-inch frame with its forty-six inch chest was no mean feat. If only his other expenses weren't so high.

Satisfied with his choices, Jordan sat at his dresser and opened the drawer. He pulled out a hand-held looking glass, the only mirror he kept in the suite—he'd even had the one in the commode room taken out when he converted the upper floor of the saloon into his office and living quarters. Jordan adjusted his tie and the eyepatch. He had once been an attractive man. Now a livid scar bisected the right half of his face from forehead to chin. The large patch hid some of the scar. The thick, neatly-trimmed full beard helped too. So did his long, carefully arranged hairstyle and the loose wide-brimmed Stetsons. Today Jordan wore the light gray hat, his favorite. He always wore his hats pulled low, indoors and out. The gray one matched the patch. A black eyepatch was too conspicuous, it made him feel like a buccaneer.

The rooms were warming up and getting stuffy. He decided to wait for the men downstairs. The bar would be their first stop anyway. He checked his pocket watch. Any time now.

Jordan was sure the thing had ended a year ago when Billy Ferson blew into town with the story. Ferson's showing up didn't surprise him, every jailbird west of the Missouri roosted at Lodgepole sooner or later. Until Billy came it was the cavern that once held an eye and the canyon that split his face that confronted Jordan with his past. Now he found himself among other faces, faces of men who had been there or heard the rumors. And Billy Ferson, slovenly, nearly incoherent Ferson, was a good one for rumors.

Billy had just come from Yuma and Jordan had little reason to doubt him. When he said the man was dead, mowed down by the Gatling gun on the prison wall, Jordan welcomed the news. The hate that simmered inside him could now be doused and the ashes buried with the man who had fanned the flames for so many months.

Until last week.

Out of nowhere came the cursed news. It was funny, the first thing that came to mind was the knowledge he'd soon have a bigger payroll to meet. For this was something that had to be taken care of immediately and no expenses could be spared. If Billy Ferson was wrong about Don Braxton's death, Jordan had to make him right. His peace of mind depended on it.

He walked along the hallway past the small unused rooms on both sides where the sporting gals once plied their trade. Most of them were gone now too and the thought saddened him. He stopped at the landing of the spiral staircase to the saloon below. It no longer surprised him to see his barroom at a quarter capacity. Any rational businessman would have cut his losses months ago, even if it meant tearing the Emporium apart stick-by-stick and selling the lumber. But Harv Jordan was no ordinary businessman. Here among the rough crowd he sensed a feeling of tolerance. In Lodgepole eccentricity was the rule not the exception.

"Mr. Jordan, sir."

He whirled to face Billy Ferson slouching in the hallway. For some reason Billy had come through the alley and up the back stairs. Jordan realized with a start he'd forgotten to lock the back door. Around here a mistake like that could be a man's last.

Billy's calico shirt was open and his beer belly spilled over his belt buckle. He reeked of whisky but at least he was still on his feet. People like these were irritating to a man of Jordan's sensibilities, but Billy was a fair shot and, thus far, had proved himself a loyal worker. The stout, dimwitted ex-con earned his pay and more just by being a good listener, and by having a pair of tightly sealed lips. He might not know what a man was talking about, but, drunk or sober, he'd often as not be able to repeat the conversation word for word.

"Yes, Billy?"

Ferson smiled that stupid snaggle-toothed grin and Jordan hoped this was a fresh drunk that could be halted and not the tail end of a bender.

"Just got in. Never ever made it so fast. Train, wow, she cover in an hour what a feller walks in a day!"

"Yes, Billy. I'm glad you enjoyed the train ride. Did you see him? He's alive?"

"And Santa Fe's such a purty town. . ."

"Goddamn it, Billy, I don't want a tourist report! Did you see Don Braxton?"

Ferson nodded. "He's out all right. Testy as ever. Shot Ernie. Killed him dead."

Jordan grasped the smaller man's shirt collar and yanked him off his feet. Just as abruptly he dropped him and turned away, ashamed he'd lost his temper. He felt genuine pain at the loss of Ernest Keppman. One of the few men here he could talk to. Crude, sure, like the others, but Ernest could be surprisingly gentle at times, and . . . maybe something could have come of it. Keppman gone. Goddamn!

Composed again, Jordan said quietly, "Aren't you going to tell me what happened?"

Ferson shrugged. " 'Pears he got Ernie 'fore Ernie could get him. A Mex slut got it somehow, too."

"And you and Franklin? Where were you and Franklin?"

"Downstairs havin' a drink. Ernie drew high card."

"What . . . what are you talking about, man?"

"Ernie drew high card. See, we was havin' such a good

time and all, figured this job only needed one of us, right? One guy, go up and bring this Braxton down. All you gotta do is point a gun and say 'come on,' right? So Ernie pulls queen of clubs and up he goes.''

Is it the crazy man who questions the imbecile? ''All right. Where is he now, Billy?''

''Boot Hill, I guess. With the Mex girl.''

''Not Keppman, you idiot, Braxton!''

Billy drew away, hurt. ''No call to talk to me like that, Boss.''

''Braxton's in jail?'' Jordan's stomach kicked over at his own words. Braxton, in jail again, out of reach once more. Maybe they'd hang him. Jordan would be sure to attend.

''In jail? Oh no, Boss, he lit out.''

''And . . . the posse went after him, did they?''

''Posse? Ain't no posse. Ain't nobody out to catch him.''

Of course not. A heavily armed stranger and a prostitute are shot. People figure something's been settled and it's just as well. ''Where's Franklin, Billy?''

Ferson nodded in the direction of the saloon below them, then pulled a comb from his pocket and ran it through greasy strands of blonde hair. Jordan looked over the patrons, spied Frank Tores leaning against the bar. Tores had accepted a glass from the barkeep and was carrying it over to a table.

''I see,'' said Jordan. ''Tores fortifies himself while you come up here to report your failure.''

''Fortifies?'' Billy was puzzled but let it pass. ''Well, it ain't really a failure, Mr. Jordan. Could've happened to anyone, you know? I mean, these things happen all the time, you know?''

Jordan gave him a kind smile. ''Sure, Billy.'' What the hell. The moron meant well. Jordan handed him a five-dollar note. ''Go have a drink, though Lord knows you've had plenty.''

''Why thanks, Mr. Jordan!'' His face beamed with anticipation. He had already lost his pay to Frank Tores.

''Now, Billy,'' Jordan assumed a fatherly tone, ''have a

good time today but tomorrow you rest up and no drinking. Franklin and I will handle any questions about Ernest, do you understand? That's very important. You don't know *anything*.'' Billy smirked and saluted him.

Jordan took four steps down the staircase and shouted, ''Tores!'' When the big man with the patch roared the room fell silent.

Frank Tores's eyes were tiny black holes in fishbelly-white skin. His face was narrow with a thin-lipped mouth, a beaky nose, and a high forehead. Long black hair parted in the middle accentuated his hatchet features. The long ride from the railhead had left a layer of trail grit on the gunman's usually immaculate kidskin duster and Jordan noticed he hadn't even bothered to dust off his black bowler hat.

''You want me, Mr. Jordan?'' He made it sound insulting. Jordan could sense his beady eyes roving the room, making sure everyone was watching. Tores was tired, a little drunk and feeling mean.

Jordan would have to be careful. ''I'd like you to come up and have a drink with me. I need to talk to you.''

Tores swaggered up the steps like a man on the way to the gallows with a mouthful of spit for the hangman. His ferret's eyes were half shut and bloodshot. He was obviously in no mood to be ridden about the fiasco in Yuma. ''So you need to talk to me, do you?'' Tores drew out his sentences, purred his words. ''You'd like me to come up and have a drink with you?'' He reached the step below Jordan and stared up into his face, swaying on his feet. ''You got some goddam business to discuss, I take it!''

Always the defiant one, the hardcase. The most useful of Jordan's men because he could think on his own. Which made him the most dangerous. There were a few others like Tores around, ones who didn't respect a man just because there was money in his pocket. Jordan wondered if maybe they sensed who and what he was.

''Later, Franklin.'' He turned on his heels and stormed down the hallway, brushing Billy Ferson aside with the swipe of an arm. He shambled into his office and locked the door. This helpless rage was a feeling he knew all too well. He unlocked the top drawer of his desk and pushed aside the small-caliber Smith & Wesson to get at the brown pharmaceutical vial. There were times—and he was painfully aware of them—when he could not live with the feelings that battered him when he dealt with certain men. Tores, that arrogant bastard with his cruel bleached face and insulting lip; the way he spoke and the way he moved, it was as if he knew and did it to mock him. Jordan unstopped the vial and forced the bitter laudanum down. It always made him gag, but the alcohol warmth floated instantly through him. And the opium in the mixture would nip at its heels.

Tores too had his fatal flaws. The fool convinced himself he worked for his pleasure and not for the money Jordan so generously doled out. Tores needed to feel he bowed to no man. But no, his real fault was not pride. It was the most dangerous weakness of all. Anyone could see it—the way Tores handled guns, the way he mechanically shot down any bird or animal unlucky enough to cross his path. The way he had goaded that drifter into drawing against him last week. Tores enjoyed killing.

Killing was his opium. Somehow the knowledge was calming. Jordan eyed the last few drops of the precious liquid. He must get to the chemist at Moab at once, try to get more. And while he was there he'd send a wire to Chang up in Salt Lake. No more opium. Damn!

And Ernest, gone forever.

Braxton! He smashed his fist on the desk top. Braxton hadn't been killed in prison, Billy had confused him with someone else. Braxton not only lived, he lived as a free man!

Jordan was no newcomer to the opiates and he knew they altered nothing but a man's outlook. Yet as the narcotic plied its subtle changes it *did* seem possible to find Braxton again. He had slipped into the vastness of the Arizona desert but no white man stayed there long. Jordan would pass the word from Kansas to California. Eventually Braxton would turn

up. Jordan picked up the pistol and ran his hands over it,
deriving confidence from its familiar weight and feel. He
rose and paced the office. Braxton would be his—*must* be
his!

   Braxton would sit before him in that plush cowhide chair.
And Jordan's ruined face would be the last thing he saw.

# Five

Benjy Thomas was sweating hard. Summer seemed unwilling to retreat this year. Mile after mile of sage and sandstone rolled by without a sign of Percy's spread and Benjy wondered if he had taken a wrong turn. It was a long ride, clear to the other side of the county, and he'd be lucky to make it back by sundown. And it sure as hell wasn't any shorter if you had no whisky.

The horses would make it worth his while. He'd admired them when he was out this way last spring, and now they were for sale at a fine price. Two stunning four-year-old mares, a chestnut and a dun. They'd make any healthy stallion lower his head, kick up his heels and sire the finest remuda stock this side of the Green River.

Benjy removed his hat and brushed off the fine red grit, knowing full well the costly tan velvet would be dirt-brown again in another half-mile. He ran his fingers through thin sand-colored hair, pried away the strands that were plastered to his forehead. He reached for his handkerchief, and made to tie it around his head. But it wouldn't reach. Instead he raised his canteen from the saddle pommel and wet the cloth, daubing the tender back of his neck. He was being fried raw by the South Utah sun. He really ought to get out in that sun a little more. For a rancher he was plenty pale, and as a result prone to sunburn.

He pulled his hat low but still had to squint as he rode. He had sparkling blue eyes topped by long flowing lashes, but today the whites of those eyes were crimson, bloodied by swollen veins. He scratched the blond stubble on his cheeks and vowed to take a shave in town soon. He never could stand the way a half-beard itched, but the thought of shaving depressed him. Last time he took a good hard look in the big parlor window he saw his handsome features marred by a kind of creeping puffiness. Bags had built up under his eyes and unless his mind was tricking him even his nose—that straight, strong never-broken nose—was swelling.

He was relieved to see the big natural arch they called Yebachi Bridge. Now there was no question he was on the right trail; he was better than halfway there. It was a cheering prospect and he patted his gentle buckskin gelding. His work and distance mount, it had a smoother gait and could get more out of its food than the pinto, but Benjy missed the flashy stallion. Riding the big paint made him feel a little taller, a little smarter, and a little richer, like walking into the Emporium with Kat. Well, the pinto was a fine sprinter, but speed on the short run didn't count for shit in this treacherous country. Hell with the fires out, someone had once called land like this. Benjy knew it as Slickrock.

If he remembered right this was the last stretch, where the trail wound along the side of the canyon and climbed to higher, wetter country. And there it was, Percy's ranch, spectacularly set among mauve sandstone fins and banded cliffs. The old man was standing out by the main corral.

"Howdy, Mr. Percy. Been waitin' long?"

"All day."

"I'm sorry, Mr. Percy, but I believe I mentioned back in Lodgepole I was a late riser."

"Well, that's your loss, boy." The old man spat a rancid chaw.

"You . . . you didn't sell 'em, did ya?"

"Fred C. Percy keeps his word," he said huffily. "If I said I'd hold them horses for you till tomorrow, that means I held 'em."

"Well I'm real pleased to hear that, Mr. Percy." Benjy dismounted. "Say, you wouldn't have somethin' to wet a man's throat now, would you?"

Percy nodded in the direction of the well.

"I was thinkin' of somethin' with a little more spirit to it," said Benjy.

"Young man, next feller runs this here ranch will do what he pleases, but long as Fred C. Percy still stands on God's acres, ain't no whisky ever gonna despoil it."

"Uh, of course, Mr. Percy." Old man, don't you change your mind about them horses! "I was thinkin' of maybe some bottled sasperilly or somethin'," he added hastily.

Percy looked at him dubiously. "You want to see them dams or what?" Benjy's head bobbed in reply. "There they be." He spat at a holding pen at the south end of the corral. "And a finer pair of breeders you ain't likely to find in this territory."

Benjy pulled out his bankroll. "I know the animals, sir, and I must say, it's a right reasonable price."

"Man does what he must," Percy mumbled.

"I'm real sorry to hear you come on hard times, Mr. Percy."

It was as if Benjy had unplugged a hole in the dam. "I been here a heap a years, boy. Beat the desert, whipped the Utes, come through the gold rush." The old man's eyes blazed. "Know what it took to force me out, son? Eh? I'll tell you. One smart city man, with his paper and pen, that's what it took." He spat a soggy clump of plug. "Yessir, that's all it takes to steal a man's land today."

"Supposin' I found a lawyer feller who said Jordan didn't

have legal right to push me off? Well, what then?'' He jabbed his finger in Benjy's chest. "Nearest law's Moab, day on the trail. And the law ain't interested in folks like me. We don't vote and we ain't got no money to give away for politickin'.''

He put his hand on Benjy's arm. "Son," he said gently, "I don't mean to criticize you. It ain't no secret you work for Mr. Jordan.''

"Man does what he must, Mr. Percy.'' Benjy handed him the money.

Percy counted it, then handed back a bill. "I don't need no charity, boy.''

"Neither do I," said Benjy, pressing the bill in his hands. "Them horses is worth more than what was agreed. You keep it, Mr. Percy.'' Benjy mounted up with the mares in tow. "Good luck, sir. We'll be real good to these critters, you'll see.'' He leaned out of the saddle to shake the gnarled hand. "Goodbye, Mr. Percy. You take care now.''

"The Lord provides for His servants, son.'' Percy watched the younger man ride into the slickrock with the prize animals. "Boy!'' he called when he was almost out of earshot. "You keep away from drink, hear? I seen many a strong man destroyed by likker, you mark me!''

But Benjy didn't catch it all. He turned and waved once, then headed down the narrow hard-packed trail, wondering if he'd make Harv's Emporium by sundown.

The route took him through eroded pinnacles and jumbled boulders. It was as if a mountain range had been taken apart piece by piece and the fragments sown over the land like seed. Balanced rocks and stone arches bore witness to the power of wind and water. Here the high desert gave little ground to vegetation. No cactus forest spread its thorny, verdant carpet over the hillsides. Instead sage, shadscale, and cliffrose clutched the gritty swells and climbed the cliffs where shrub-like juniper took root in cracks in the rock. Along the trail the tiny, densely-packed flowers of golden rabbitbrush made a liar of a sun that swore summer was still here.

Benjy didn't need bright autumn blooms to tell him winter was on the way. Already the evenings held out the threat of frost. That was another reason he wanted to make town before dark. He wasn't dressed for cool weather.

And he wasn't ready for his grating nerves and trembling hands. As the day wore on the morning's drinks wore off, paving the way for the full onslaught of the hangover from last night's drinking bout. He had to follow the sun across the sky and the glare made his eyeballs sizzle. He'd still be on the trail by the time that damned hunk of fire finally ducked behind the Escalantes.

At last he reached the flimsy rope and plank bridge over the Dirty Devil. Wagging his head, he dismounted. Couldn't recall crossing it this morning but he must have, there was no other route. He stared into the crevice. His gaze followed the layers of vermillion sandstone and purple shale and fell on the turbid river a thousand feet below.

He swallowed hard, took a step onto the bridge and felt his breakfast turn over. Another step and the bridge swayed ominously. He clutched the rope holds. The damn bridge was dancing! His wobbly legs were the culprit. And these horses would have to be led across, one at a time.

Impossible.

Why did the sight of that boiling river fill him with such dread? What was he, some shaver traipsin' through a graveyard on a stormy night? He took some deep breaths, took hold of the reins, and ventured out. His legs nearly buckled. He shut his eyes and his head started spinning. Hellfire! Once he crossed that river he could be at the bar in two hours. Better to perish in those muddy rapids below than die here on the rim of a hangover! Not daring to breathe, he led the first horse out.

It was well past sundown when he hitched the three animals to the post in front of the saloon, and he paused on the street side of the batwings to pull himself together. It wouldn't do to go staggering in. It wouldn't do at all. A man who showed such weakness here in Lodgepole was rightful prey. Head held high, Benjy Thomas strode through the saloon up to the bar.

"Howdy, Red," he said to the big Irish barkeep. "Got any of that aged Kentucky left?" Red McKormick came up with the last of the Emporium's bourbon. "I'll take the bottle, my good man."

"Hey, Thomas, you in a sportin' mood tonight?" Benjy turned to the familiar voice. Frank Tores, Billy Ferson, and a third fellow he didn't know sat at a corner table.

"Aw, come on, Benjy," said Ferson. "Three-handed ain't much fun."

Benjy loved poker almost as much as he loved whisky. If he got up from a game breaking even he considered himself ahead—he'd played for free. Tonight he carried more money than usual. He meant to make a payment this morning on the way out to Percy's but hadn't been able to rouse Jordan. He could let that slide if he had to. Or maybe take it out in trade.

The whisky was refreshing. He felt lucky again and he held his glass high. "To Fred C. Percy," he said. He was glad Percy was moving on peacefully. He would hate to be sent out there with Tores to "have a talk with him." Benjy sure didn't cotton to crowding a man like Percy off his land. But he didn't nose into other folks' affairs either. You couldn't, if you wanted to live long.

"Dealer's choice." Tores shuffled for the cut.

Benjy brought his glass and bottle over to the table and sat in the one vacant chair. "Suits me. Say, boys, before we start, couple a hours is it for me. Had a long day on the trail. Got me them two mares."

"Can't keep a filly waitin' for her stud, eh, Thomas?"

Billy chimed in. "Shit, I wouldn't even be here if I had that to go home to."

Benjy's grin flagged. "Come on boys, you know I don't take to ribbin' about Kat."

Tores smirked. "Sure, Thomas, don't get steamed. Let's play cards. My game's five-card draw. Pair of knaves or better starts the bettin'." He dealt.

"So when you boys get in from Arizona?" Benjy asked pleasantly.

"Saturday," Tores grunted, studying his hand.

"Ever been on a train, Benjy?" Billy asked. "Wee-oh! They are *fast*!"

Benjy gathered his cards and looked them over. "Let's open with ten bucks. Where's Ernie these days?"

Billy shot Tores a look. "Dead," Tores said.

"No shit! What happened?"

"Drunk Navajo."

Benjy shook his head. "Damn. Injuns and likker. Gimme two cards, Frank. Catch the bugger?"

Billy nodded. "Hung him, didn't we, Frank?"

This was a surprise to Tores. He had to admit it was a nice touch. The dummy's getting pretty good, makin' up his own lies. "That's right," he purred. "That buck was so drunk he just laughed and laughed. Poor bastard even laughed when we put the noose around his neck. Laughed till he dropped."

The stairs groaned under a heavy footfall and the cardplayers turned in their seats. Harv Jordan walked towards them. Tores looked at Billy and rolled his eyes skyward.

Jordan stopped at their table. "Hello, boys." The big man stood tall and straight, appearing even more massive than usual. Tores tapped his cards into a neat pile and placed them face down on the table. He slid his chair out, leaned back on two legs and stared up into Jordan's face.

"I ain't ready to have that talk yet," Tores said.

"I didn't come here for that, Frank. I just wanted to see how you boys are doing. Sir . . ." he addressed the fourth man. "I don't believe I've had the pleasure."

"Charlie Boston," the man said. "Provo."

Jordan touched the brim of his Stetson. "Harv Jordan. Columbia, South Carolina. Welcome to Lodgepole, Charlie. I see you're back in town, Benjy. It's been a while."

Tores broke in. "Godamighty, aren't we friendly tonight!"

Jordan ignored him. "What's the news with you, Benjy?"

"Uh, I seen Mr. Percy today," Benjy mumbled after some hesitation. "I reckon he'll be moving on soon."

"Here's my ten," said Tores. He tossed a greenback into the pile and the others followed.

"He agreed to be off the ranch next week then, did he?" Jordan inquired. Benjy hid his eyes in his cards while he lied with a nod of his head. "That's good, that's good," said Jordan. "How's the old coot taking it?"

Benjy pretended he hadn't heard. "Opener takes three cards," was what he said.

Jordan began to shift his weight from one foot to the other and back. "He will be out, then?" he persisted. Tores dealt the draw and Benjy picked up his new cards and arranged them in his hand.

"He's an old man, Mr. Jordan." Benjy spoke quietly. "You know how old men are. They tend to slowness and forgettin'."

"Ah well, a day or two won't make a difference," said Jordan brightly. His voice held a strange detached quality, like a man who would slur his words if he had one more drink. Suddenly Jordan clapped his huge hands together. "A poor night to talk business, eh fellows?" he boomed. He dipped into his breast pocket and pulled out a handful of fat, rich-smelling Havanas. "Anyone like one? I have extras."

"Gee thanks, Boss!" Billy rose from his chair and reached across the table for the cigar. Tores grabbed hold of his arm and pulled him back into his seat.

"Stay put, Billy." He turned to Charlie Boston. "Billy's eyes got the wanderlust," he explained.

"Aw heck, Frank, I wouldn't cheat. You know I wouldn't."

"I know nothin' of the sort. If you're about to be hangin' all over the damn table say a word first so's we can hold our cards close."

"I'd sure like one of those cee-gars," piped Benjy. "Uh, long as you've no objection to my smokin' it later."

"It's yours to do with as you please." And Jordan dropped the smokes onto the table. "And now I would like to. . ."

Tores snorted. "Why the hell you in such a good mood, Jordan? Just shoot a puppy?"

Charlie Boston cleared his throat loudly. "Boys, I think maybe I ought to be cashing in. I'm a little behind so's I can't see how anyone would object."

"No no, Charlie, stick around!" Tores was just warming up. "Mr. Jordan's a real fun guy, isn't he, Billy? Billy tell Charlie here what a fun guy Mr. Jordan is."

Billy wanted no part of it. "Aw, come on, Frank. . ."

Jordan would give it one more try though his mood was already turning around. He did want company tonight, even if part of that company had to be Tores, but if this kept up one of his dread headaches would be here too. And then there'd be nothing for it but to sleep the next ten or twelve hours. He reached into his waistcoat and pulled out a modest bankroll. "Any objections if I try my luck?"

"There's a chair, Boss. I'll get it." And Billy rose, only to be jerked roughly back into his seat.

"Wha'd I just tell you 'bout that shit, Billy?" Tores snarled.

"He was just goin' for a chair, Frank," said Benjy.

Tores ignored him and looked Jordan straight in the face. "I'd just as soon you found another game, Mr. Jordan," he said sweetly. "You know how confused I get by five-handed poker."

"Really," said Charlie. "I ought to be going. I got a very long ride north." He made to rise.

"You always hit the trail at night, Charlie?" snapped Tores. "Stay where you are."

Jordan worked his head from side to side as if looking for something. This situation, suddenly and unaccountably, was confusing, unreal. Jordan had an inexplicable urge to check his eyepatch, to reassure himself it was still there. He settled for adjusting his hat. "Well, I only wanted to play for an hour or so," he managed to say.

"Well . . . all right, Mr. Jordan," Tores purred. "It does make for bigger pots, don't it boys? Tell you, though, Mr. Jordan, this is dealer's choice, and I like to play the game with wild cards. That O.K. by you?"

"Why sure, Frank, dealer's choice." Jordan took a step towards the empty chair at a nearby table.

"Right then," said Frank Tores. "One-eyed jacks are wild."

No one laughed. Jordan stood still. Billy shifted in his seat. Charlie Boston coughed, this time for real because he had swallowed his cigarette smoke. Benjy poured a drink and drained it.

Jordan spoke first, slowly, without turning to look at them. "I do know of a game near here. The company there is . . . amenable." Mustering his dignity he now pivoted to face them. "Gentlemen, I bid you goodnight," and he lumbered away. They all watched as he walked out the door and into the street. The bounce was gone from his step.

"Jesus, Frank!" It was Benjy. Billy Ferson was still speechless.

Tores chuckled. "Wants us to think he's got a game over at Hadley's. All right let's play some goddam cards. Dealer takes two."

"Forget it, Billy. Here's my ten. Dealer takes two."

Benjy took it easy. He wanted the bottle to last. The game was agreeable enough, not enough money changed hands for anyone to get sore. And that was the trouble. Benjy grew impatient and frustrated. The cards were falling his way and he couldn't collect on them. Lord knew a little extra cash would make things easier with Kat. She was edgy lately. Went through the books and was wondering at some of the things she found. Now she wanted to hire a roundup crew, put in stores, have a gander at the title to the ranch.

It was way off there, on the horizons of his mind. He didn't like to look but when he did he could see the storm coming. Maybe not today or tomorrow, but it was coming. And he knew damn well how fast a storm can move.

"Boys, it's late," Benjy said. "And I still got to be gettin' out to the ranch."

"Sure, Thomas," Tores agreed. "How 'bout one more go-round?"

Benjy nodded. He held up his bottle, sloshed the few remaining ounces. "This ain't worth takin' home. Anybody?" Billy held out his glass. Benjy split the rest of the bourbon between them and picked up his hand. Two pairs, queens and nines. Not bad. "I'll open it up with fifty," he said. What the hell.

"Too rich for my blood," said the man Benjy didn't know.

"Me too. I'm out." Billy tossed his cards face down on the table.

"Well then, Thomas, it's just you and me," said Tores pleasantly. "Here's your fifty and I'll kick it up eighty."

Eighty? Benjy only had a couple hundred on him. Two high pairs, though. He counted out the money and placed it on the table. "All right, I'll see it. Give me one card."

"One card," Tores repeated, and dealt it. "Dealer stands pat."

"No cards!" gushed Billy.

Benjy studied his opponent's face for a clue. Nothing. Shit. He picked up his card. Another queen! Full house. Damn tough hand to beat. "Opener bets one hundred dollars."

"See your hundred and raise you two hundred," said Tores.

"Wow!" Ferson exclaimed.

"Frank, I'm tapped out. Will you take a marker?"

"Shall we be polite about this, or do I laugh in your face?" Cough up or fold."

The rest of Benjy's bankroll stood outside at the hitching rail, waiting to make him and Kat the finest horse breeders on either side of the Green. Benjy looked down at the excellent hand he held. A man does what he must. "I'll see it and call."

"Where's your money, Thomas?"
"Come on outside and I'll show you," said Benjy.


If the heat ever got the kid down he didn't show it. Brax
would have taken to shade by one o'clock but Vicente knew
how to best pace man and horse. While they followed the
Colorado upstream Brax would plunge in every hour or so
and ride cool until his clothes dried, about ten minutes. Game
was scarce in the low country but the channel cats were
running fat and lazy, and a little south of Needles, Vicente
bagged a javelina. He removed the musk gland in the
hindquarters and dressed the beast, and they pit-broiled it in a
canyon paradise of palms and sycamore. If any Louisiana
porker ever tasted so good Brax couldn't remember when.
All in all, this hotheaded Mexican proved a most useful
companion. He showed Brax how to stretch their meager
coffee supply with jojoba beans and introduced him to an
Indian delicacy, roast tail of chuckwalla. He could skin and
cook a rattlesnake in minutes. One day Brax saw him bring
down a quail in flight with his rifle at forty yards.
    Vicente was a hell of a yarnspinner too. With his careful,
precise English he could tell a ghost story to send Brax
huddling under the covers with a wide grin on his face. He
talked about his life in Mexico where a scholarly Franciscan
monk had instilled in him a love of books and had actually
encouraged truck with the American drifters in order to
master their language. And when the good Brother Salcido
didn't have him Vicente's half-uncle did. Swimming Wolf
was a full-blooded Mescalero Apache whose dream was to
pass his lifetime of knowledge on to his nephew in the few
years he had left. Brax was impressed with the product of
these two very different teachers. Few men read trail sign and
books equally well.
    But all that Vicente got out of his companion was that he
hailed from East Texas and had fought in the war. Brax didn't
mention that he'd been starved, bayonetted and shot twice.

After the war, Brax said, he drove cattle up the Pecos Trail. It took him West and he stayed. Vicente figured this last bit of information was meant to account for the years since the War Between the States, and he didn't push for more.

In the afternoons they watched late summer clouds dapple the land with huge patches of shadow. Some days, on the edges of a dazzling blue sky, they could see thunderheads trailing braids of rain across the thirsty plains. One evening, Vicente pulled a large folded document out of his saddlebag and spread the yellowed paper in the light of the campfire.

Brax hunkered down beside him. "What you got there, kid?"

"Arizona Territory, some of Utah." The map was out of date and showed no railroads and only the older trails, but it accurately placed the timeless features of the land. "Brother Salcido gave it to me. Here," he pointed. "El Cañon Grande. We must go around it."

"Ever seen the Canyon?"

"No. But I am sure only birds and angels can cross it."

"Where's this Lodgepole? Lodgepole on that map?"

Vicente studied the paper and located the necessary mountain ranges. He came up with a pencil, did a little figuring and put a prominent X on the map. "It is now, Señor."

Morning found them in a vast, bowl-shaped valley that looked like it had been scraped clean. The far horizons on all sides were sawtoothed with spires and buttes. An oblong mesa broke the foreground by rearing its table-flat head three hundred feet above the desert floor. Only dunebroom and sage anchored the low hills of coarse reddish sand that filled the rest of the basin.

And the northern sky was ominous. Murky thunderheads thousands of feet high rolled and traded lightning bolts. The sun winked out, shadows vanished and the pink sand seemed to glow with a light of its own. It was hot. Hotter than ever, it seemed, because of the mugginess. There was the smell of water—the air was saturated but the boiling black sky wouldn't part with its rain. And there was the peculiar odor of ozone. The captive lightning made the hair on the back of their necks stand straight, and the horses were nervous. They had to coax the skittish beasts at a walk.

Brax wiped the streaming sweat from his eyes. "Don't like this place," he muttered.

"It is the high desert of the Navajo, Señor Brax."

Ahead a wall of water joined sky and earth. "Cloudburst. I'm not anxious to ride into that."

"But the storm seems determined to meet us."

This wasn't the first thunderstorm to pass through today. The pungent scent of wet sage was a dead giveaway and they could hear the roar of runoff crashing through the draws and canyons that dissected the oval plateau a few hundred yards away. Brax pointed to the mesa. "Need be, we'll lay over by those cliffs."

"The Navajo, he is peaceful, no?"

Brax shrugged. "Anyone peaceful these days?" It drew a knowing smile. "If I remember it right," Brax continued, "Kit Carson trounced them good, back in the sixties at De Chelly. Government penned 'em up at the Bosque Redondo, then turned 'em loose here." He scanned the barren scene. "White man don't want this land. Hell, cactus don't even like it here."

"I have heard the Navajo is a most enthusiastic horse thief."

"What Indian ain't?" Brax replied. "I heard they keep to themselves."

"I hope you are right. Because they are up on the mesa right now and they seem very interested in us."

Brax followed the end of Vicente's outstretched arm to the cliff tops. His eyes caught a flash of movement, then there was nothing. "We're out in the open," he observed.

"If we must run, we should go to the cliffs."

"The *cliffs?* That's where the buggers are hiding!"

"If we turn tail we are in range even longer. The rocks are safest."

"*If* we can get there! I'm not sure if that line of reasoning makes sense to me, Vicente."

The horses plodded on. Vicente did not take his eyes from the mesa. "Then you suggest?" he said at last.

"Well for now, keep going, tend to our own affairs." Brax pulled up on the reins. "Hey, what are you doing, kid?"

He was taking the Winchester from his saddle boot. He pumped the lever to send a cartridge into the chamber. "My affairs include staying alive," he reminded Brax.

Brax grunted. "Know any Navajo?" Vicente shook his head. "Me neither." He cupped his hands around his mouth. "You there!" he shouted. "Come on down and parry!" Turning to his companion he said, "Maybe they're just hungry. We got a little extra. . ."

The thick wet atmosphere muffled the crack of the rifle shot but the bullet was close enough to spit dirt at their feet. Vicente raised the Winchester to his shoulder and answered with three fast rounds.

The hesitation was in his face to be read as Brax looked over the ground to be crossed. But the second shot from the mesa was so close he swore he could feel its wind and that settled it right then. They burst into a dead run. Lightning flashed, another shot was echoed by the thunder and the Navajos cut loose with all they had. Rifle fire exploded all around them; the very sky was hailing lead. It was an endless gauntlet. The frightened horses surged ahead at full speed but, as in a nightmare, the mesa seemed to skitter further away with each pounding step. Brax heard the whine of a bullet as it ricocheted, saw the scar appear as if by magic on the saddle pommel where it hit. He hugged the horse's neck and put his spurs to her flanks but the gray was giving it all she had.

Vicente reined up under cover of the rocks but Brax overshot him, the mare veered to the left and thundered along the side of the mesa towards the Indians. Horrified, Brax tried to turn her while his friend peppered the cliffs with rifle fire.

The Navajos scurried and Brax finally managed to spin the horse on its hindquarters and get himself out of the line of fire.

They had found refuge in one of the many canyons that split the plateau. From above a projecting ledge shielded them and they were protected on the front and sides by piled boulders. Across the canyon and hundreds of feet above them were the Indians—well-rested, well-armed, and patient.

"How many?" panted Brax. "Eight? Ten?"

"Two or three," Vicente said flatly. "And I think they want our horses." A shot screamed off the rocks and he dove for cover. On the walls above an Indian appeared and Vicente leaped to his feet, rifle at the shoulder, and drew a bead. Before he could fire Brax knocked the weapon to the side.

"There's got to be a better way," said Brax, but Vicente just stared at him as though he'd lost his mind. The world flickered once and rumbled. "Storm's right overhead now," Brax observed.

"What do you suggest we do, surrender?"

"Indian war's been over this part of the Territory for years."

"Tell *them* that!" Vicente snarled. "Shall we turn over our mounts? How far do you think it is to next water?"

"Listen, Vicente. Those bucks up there, think they're on foot?"

Vicente nodded. "Only a man or a burro could get up there. But you have not answered my question, my peace-loving friend. What do you intend . . ." Suddenly he clapped his hands together. "Of course!"

"Now hold on, I'm still trying to hatch this so don't you go off half-baked. . ."

But Vicente would hear none of it. He thrust the rifle into Brax's hands. "Keep their heads down," he instructed. Brax threw a few potshots into the cliffs and the braves disappeared. "That's it, Señor Brax. Keep it up." Brax fired a few more times. When he turned back to his companion he was gone.

Vicente worked his way downstream, out of the canyon to the outermost wall of the mesa. If the entire network of draws was as steep and sheer-walled as this one it was certain the braves had gained the summit on foot. And that meant that somewhere, on the far side of the mesa, Vicente would have to circle around the long way. He hugged the cliffs as he picked his way along the walls, ducking behind rocks and scanty trees until he reached a gap where the crevice opened into the heart of the mesa. It was forty yards to the safety of the thick brush and jumbled boulders on the other side. He'd make a fine target crossing that.

Brax waited in the rocks. He waited for Vicente, for the Navajos, for the rain. The kid sure didn't waste any time on talk, didn't believe in jaw-flapping when action was called for. Up there, across the canyon, something was moving. The sky flashed and excused itself with a roll of thunder. The movement, there it was again. Brax aimed high, but close enough to make the Indian think twice about showing himself a third time.

Vicente tossed a stone across the gap and it didn't draw a shot. Then the roar of fast rifle fire drifted his way. Brax had picked a good time to keep them busy. A rope of flame twisted across the sky and the heavens opened up. Raindrops plunged to the ground so hard that mud splashed up. Vicente dashed into the rain. At once the canyon bottoms turned to slime and he lost his footing and went down. He scrambled to his feet and almost bumped into them—two Indian ponies grazing placidly under a rock terrace.

One was a sorrel, the other white with some gray. Better than he dared hope. One dark, one light, just like his and Brax's. And because of the storm visibility was poor. Vicente took the horses by their rawhide bits and led them back along the route he had come.

With his pistol in one hand and a willowy cottonwood branch in the other he pointed the animals towards the open desert. He brought the switch down on their rumps as he fired. They bolted into the sage, past the draw where Brax

was holed up, past the Indians on their high-ground perch.
Brax heard the braves whoop at the prospect of a rousing
chase and watched them high-tail it over the mesa to the other
side.

"Mount up!" Vicente shouted as he ran, but Brax was
already in the saddle, holding the reins of his friend's roan.
They were long gone by the time the Navajos discovered the
two white men hadn't freed their own horses to save their
necks.


The morning brought a chill and though Brax couldn't prove
it by the map, as far as he was concerned this meant they were
out of Arizona. That night they made camp on a grassy
tableland high above the red desert. Vicente pointed to a peak
looming against the northeastern sky. It wore a small cap of
snow; at the mountain's base, where pinyon and juniper gave
way to Ponderosa Pine and Douglas Fir, was a spot of bare
land.

"Lodgepole."

"You sure?"

"Si. The peak stands alone, as I have been told, and the
town faces the setting winter sun. That cleared area is it,
Señor Brax."

"How far, kid?"

"An hour, maybe two." Aimlessly Brax poked at the
crackling sticks of juniper that kept them warm. "Señor
Brax, you have been quiet since our little adventure with the
Navajos. You have been working on a plan of action, no?"

Brax scowled. "Well I suppose I'll ride in careful, have a
looksee."

"No," Vicente corrected. "*I* will 'ride in careful and have
a looksee.' It is not likely I will be remembered. And it is less
likely you will be forgotten."

"I guess there's no sense in pushing things. But I can't see
how you're going to find out much."

"And neither can I, since I don't know what it is I am to find out. Señor Brax, I am not one to pry into a man's affairs, but now we have arrived and we must make some decisions." He paused to let it carry greater weight. Brax knew he was waiting for an answer. So he shrugged.

"You have been in prison, no?" Before he could reply Vicente pointed to Brax's wrist. "A man does not get such scars driving cattle. He gets them wearing chains."

Like stars at dusk the dim lights of the half-dead town appeared on the mountainside. A waning sliver of moon drifted out of the clouds while a noisy pair of pinyon jays scrapped over the leftover dinner morsels by the fire.

"A vendetta, perhaps?" Vicente pressed. "It is said many in Lodgepole have been in prison."

Brax avoided his eyes. "Don't know any more about the place than you told me," he mumbled. They unrolled their beds under a stand of pinyon and stoked the fire to fend off the chill of high-country autumn.

"Say kid, I'd feel better if we slept in shifts tonight."

"I was going to insist. This fire can be seen a long way off."

"Leave it burn. Nippy up here." Brax rose. " 'Sides, I'll be needing coffee for first watch."

Vicente held up his hand. "Sleep. I will wake you when the Great Dipper is over that mesa."

# Six

"But couldn't we get the law to take them back?"

"The *what?*" Benjy Thomas pulled a Remington revolver from his breechband. "Kat, *this* is the law around here."

"It's just that I don't take to this sneaking up on a person's camp. It's dangerous."

"It's simple as churnin' butter," he snorted, waving the pistol. "We get the drop on those varmints they ain't goin' up against us. Sane man won't risk his ass over stock that ain't his to begin with."

"You're sure that's them up there?"

He sighed. "Kat, I seen *our* horses standin' up there at the edge of the clearing."

"Well what do you want me to do?"

"I told you! What I want you to do is stand in the bushes and point that rifle. Just back me up. One of the fellers is awake, so you got to back me up. 'Case he squawks." Benjy pointed in the direction of the hill. "Just you think on those cusses, way they lead our horses away, bold as you please, while I was walking around town tryin' to work us up a crew.

Look how they sleep, innocent as babes, and we're out all that money. Why, they got those mounts all saddled up and ready. Wouldn't surprise me a bit if they was branded too, what with Percy not puttin' his mark on 'em. If you want me to take this on alone, just say so. 'Course, the snoozin' feller just might roll over shooting, if you get my drift . . .'' He'd had his say, and now he lengthened his strides, up the long slope to the camp.

What was she doing slinking through the woods like some reservation-jumping renegade? Kat had been wondering about a lot of things lately. Sure Benjy treated her fine, but she shouldn't be out here in the night like a rustler; she belonged at home in a warm kitchen with the smell of bread rising on the cookstove, the windows thrown wide so she could hear the laughter of children. Children, not drunken men who acted like children.

Lord knew she wanted to do her share of the work. But when Benjy found her tending to the stock or some such chores he'd chase her back into the house. "Men's work!" he'd scold. She should be in the house. God, how the man loved that house! Drunk or sober he'd sit by the big south window and find some kind of peace in the world. And that was the trouble with Benjy.

Sure it was rough when John died, but Kat didn't think she was the kind of woman to fall into a man's arms at the first hint of a chill wind. No, it was the romantic in Benjy that attracted her back then. But now she could see him for what he was. A loser. Charming, yes, but a loser all the same. A man who dreamed his life away, felt things were bound to turn out all right somehow. Had to turn out right because he wanted them to.

And the ranch, John Harris's dream? It was sliding down-hill. Breeding stock couldn't make up the losses. Oh, once in a while Benjy showed up with a buyer or a little money from God-knew-where, but it barely kept the larder full. You needed *real* money to make payroll, whip the place back into shape. It took money to make money, surely that was an easy lesson. One Benjy didn't seem to understand. Now Kat didn't even know how much she owned. Benjy had mislaid the title, or so he claimed. She didn't know what to believe anymore. Two years ago the man had come as a savior. Now the ranch was falling apart, *they* were falling apart, and Benjy was falling into the bottom of a bottle.

His words broke her thoughts. "There's the camp."

"I see it now," she whispered.

"Do like I said and we'll have our horses back in no time. With nobody hurt." He leaned over and pecked her cheek. She was thankful for the darkness which hid her tears.


Brax's snores mingled with the sounds of the night while Vicente huddled by the fire. He pulled his blanket tightly around him. He did not enjoy these cool evenings. He lit a stale Bull Durham, the last of the pouch except for two smokes' worth for Brax's watch. It was good. Tobacco was a luxury and a treat to be savored. Brother Salcido had frowned on the use of the weed and Uncle Swimming Wolf never seemed to bring enough for the two of them on their long summer journeys. Vicente stared into the mountain night. He drew warmth from the precious tobacco and solace from the man who slept near him. It was no matter what Brax had done to land him in prison, he was now Vicente's friend. Perhaps his only one. He was a loner. He had spent more time with characters in books than with real people and he had roamed more deserts than living rooms. Maybe that was why he was so eager to be fooled by Rosa.

With a shock he realized he hadn't thought of her since back on the trail, by the Colorado. Which hurt more: the fact of her death or the knowledge of what she had become?

This man Brax. A convict yes, but no murderer. Surely he killed when he had to, and sometimes he didn't when he should have. And now Vicente was just like him, a man

without a future. Once again he blessed the memory of his
parents, for he knew he had seen too much of this great
country to the north ever to feel at home again in the villages
of Chihuahua. The ignorance and poverty of those places
seemed far behind him now. And the death of Rosa had
severed his last ties with that narrow world. For better or
worse his fate was tied to this convict snoring away the
high-country night, this man who was at least partly responsible for Rosa's death. Ah but God works, and the world
turns, in strange ways. Vicente heard a horse snort. A twig
snapped and he whirled, rifle at the ready. But the click of a
cocked hammer froze him.

"Best put down the iron, friend." The stocky man stepped
from the bushes. His revolver was steady and aimed at
Vicente's heart. "Now you'll want to let go that gunbelt."

The blankets parted and Brax was up with his Colt. The
intruder fired hastily and the shot kicked dirt in Brax's eyes.
But there was no second shot. He could see that big Colt in
Brax's hand wasn't about to miss.

"Drop it!" Brax shouted. "It's a standoff!"

"It ain't," the man said. "My partner's got you covered.
Shoot and you both die."

Brax looked to the shadows, spotted the rifle poking from
the bushes. His gun hand shivered spilling the Colt to the
dust. The shape in the darkness lowered the rifle and took up
the reins of Brax's mare. No horse was worth your life. In the
desert maybe, but not here.

Vicente fumed. Thinking again, when he should have been
watching and listening! Many a time Brother Salcido had
rapped his knuckles for daydreaming. "We have no money
and little food," he said sullenly. "If you doubt me search for
yourself."

"Oh we will. You there." He waved the gun at Brax.
"Out of bed please. Over there with the greaser so's I can get
a good look at you. Mex, you throw another stick on that
sorry-lookin' fire, eh?"

Take the damn horses, Brax started to say as Vicente
stoked the fire and the bandit stepped into the light. Instead
his jaw dropped and all that came out was a wordless croak.

Years, pounds, and whiskers can turn an old friend into a
stranger, but not this one. Brax knew him the moment the fire
stripped the shadows from his round boyish face. Now Brax
too was in the light, and Benjy's big dancing eyes widened
even more. He tossed his gun to the ground. "Brax!" he
shouted as he threw his arms around him. "My God, I can't
believe it! It's Brax! *Brax!*" Vicente scooped up the gun and
stood holding it, not knowing quite what to do, while Benjy
pulled Brax to his feet. "Look, Kat, it's Brax! My old
partner, Don Braxton!"

The woman stepped out of the shadows. She was stunning.
Brax looked her over while Benjy pumped his hand and
blubbered. She had rosy cheeks and full lips. A bun of
straw-blonde hair was piled high under her Montana-peak
hat. Large eyes of robin's-egg blue leaped out of her tawny
face, holding Brax's gaze against his will.

The rigors of frontier life hadn't stolen this gal's youth,
unlike other women Brax had known. No frail, petite creature this one; even the baggy trail jeans and ankle-length
duster couldn't hide that ample well-proportioned figure.
Brax realized he was staring and turned away, but not before
their eyes met straight on. Had her face flushed?

"Kat, meet Brax! Brax, you ain't said nothin'. Ain't you
surprised to see me?"

"I sure am, Benjy. I'm surprised as hell."

"Well, you always was the quiet one!" Benjy guffawed.
"Now me, I'm the loudmouth. Lord I am pleased to see
you!"

"Me too, Benjy." He pushed Vicente forward. "This
here's my friend Vicente Alvarez."

Vicente still held the gun. Benjy grasped his empty hand
and Vicente nodded coolly. "Señor Benjy," he acknowledged.

"And here's my darlin' Katheryn. Kat, meet Don Braxton, one of the finest gents ever to cross the Pecos."

Brax was grateful for another chance to look at her. "It's a real pleasure, Ma'am." He meant it. She smiled and lowered her eyes. "Well, Benjy," he said quickly. "Seems things don't change much. Looking to take our horses, eh?"

Katheryn spoke crossly. "Benjy, you told me these were the horses you bought from Mr. Percy."

"Ah, mistakes happen, honey. Now that I seen the critters up close and plain, can't see how I made such a mistake. Firelight made the gray look like a dun, I reckon." He clapped his hands and threw a beefy arm around Brax's shoulders. "Plenty time to look for horse thieves tomorrow, eh buddy? What's a couple of dumb ol' horses when a friend comes back from the dead? Word was you was killed, you know."

"Like you say, mistakes happen."

"They sure do. Let's go on over to the ranch. Honey, will you rustle these gents up some grub?"

"I'd be honored to have you," she said to Brax.

"I am sorry, Señora. I am not so honored." Vicente turned to Brax. "Señor Brax, I do not find your friend here so amusing. He is a"—dove into the pool of his English and dredged it up—"would-be horse thief."

For the first time since they met he saw something like rage flare in Brax's face. "This man saved my life more than once," he almost shouted. "Man who rides with me rides with him too."

"I'm sorry," Vicente muttered.

"Yeah, well me too." And he was. Benjy had been a good friend once but by now Brax figured he knew a little about time and men.

Benjy laughed. "Forget it! Been called better by worse men." He offered his hand. "How 'bout it, kid?"

Vicente shook his hand but Brax sensed his reluctance. "Please, Señor," he mumbled, "do not call me 'keed.' "

"Well, amigo," Brax said with forced cheer, "let's break camp, eh?"

"Wait till you see that ranch house," Benjy gushed. "No stable suite for my pal, no sir!"

Benjy lead the way on the buckskin gelding. He rambled on for a while but trailed off. Tension hovered over them. Katheryn was silent and no one was willing to invade her thoughts, least of all Brax. He watched the broad back of his old friend. Benjy hadn't lost all his good looks but there were deep moats around those once-sparkling blue eyes. His face still needed little excuse to break into a wide grin but his teeth were badly stained from smoke and cut plug. And a roll of fat thickened his middle; though a few inches shy of six feet he looked to be topping two hundred pounds. Brax had never known him to tip the scales at more than one-seventy. Benjy's hands were soft and uncallused. Benjy might own a ranch but Brax had the feeling he broke more seals on bottles than he did broncs.

Benjy reined up at the crest of the ridge and pointed. "There she be, boys."

The broad, gently rolling valley below seemed to swallow all the buildings but one. In the crisp starlight the ranch house stood proudly, its back to the rocky slopes. The front door commanded a sweeping view across a small dusty yard and out, over miles of well-watered range that ran up into the juniper and oak of the far hills. It was an impressive L-shaped structure of split logs, with high walls and pitched roofs. The roofs extended past the walls to cover south- and east-facing porches. As Brax's eyes adjusted to the half-light of the open country he made out the bunkhouse and beyond that a sizeable barn with pens and corrals nearby. There were shade-trees and windbreaks and several wells. This was no hard-scrabble setup.

"Only runnin' about a hundred head or so now," Benjy explained. "But we run a string of light horses as a sideline. As fine a bunch as you're likely to see."

"Looks great, Benjy." Brax shook his head. "Funny, way things turn out. Never figured you for a rancher."

"Why not? This here's the finest ranch by far in the county. Ask anyone. And this is a pretty damn big county."

"Well I sure didn't expect to find you still in Lodgepole."

"And I didn't expect to see you again, ever. What bring you boys up this way anyhow? Pretty long haul from, uh, South Arizona. . ."

"We heard there was gold here," Vicente piped up.

He burst into a hearty horse-laugh. "So did I, boy, so did I. I was a couple of months too late, but you two are goin' on a couple of years. Tell you, Brax, I didn't think I'd be here long either, when I seen what slim pickin's there was to be had." He pranced his mount back to where Katheryn waited, took the reins from her and pulled the horse around so she faced them. "But I did find gold, and here she is. See, Kat's first husband, a fine gent by the name of John Harris, he died leavin' this here ranch. A place like this, a place like this needs a *man,* Brax, and along comes I. Plenty lucky for both of us, eh honey?"

Brax eyed the sprawling house. Harris must have been a man of considerable means, and he must have liked his comforts.

The front door opened into the kitchen, a cheerful orderly place where spice racks, peg boards, and utensils were crowded along yellow walls. Everything was efficiently arranged: the big woodburner, countertop cabinets, a cache of pots for stew, basins for cleanup. The other half of the room was lost to the kitchen table and four dowel-back chairs.

"Fellows hungry?" Kat asked as they sat. She spun about a few times opening and closing cabinets and suddenly the counter in front of her littered with pots and pans. "I'll scramble up a dozen eggs or so for starters. Benjy, will you go fetch 'em please?"

"Uh, Ma'am . . . Benjy, if it's all the same I'd sooner pass on that."

"What's that, Brax? You ain't hungry?" said Benjy.

"Why I'd bet dung to doughnuts you boys ain't had but hardtack and jerky all month."

"Partner, right now a couple hours' shuteye'd do me better than vittles."

"I also thank you for your generous offer, but like Señor Brax I prefer to sleep with a light stomach."

"Now if that offer was to stand for breakfast . . ." Brax added with a grin.

" 'Course it does," said the woman firmly. "I'll just leave everything out. Skillets don't spoil."

"Kat, honey grab me my bottle off the shelf." She hedged at Benjy's request but whatever it was that flashed across her face was quickly replaced by a smile.

"Now that's a different story," said Brax. "Sip or two before bed makes for pleasant dreams."

Benjy accepted the bottle. Kat stood behind the fourth chair. Benjy uncorked the bottle. "I won't be long, Kat," he said.

She didn't move.

Brax spoke up. "Been a while since I've had anyone to talk to, 'sides the kid and myself." He looked at Vicente and grinned. "Still ain't sure which of us is worse company." Vicente sprang to his feet and pulled out the chair for Kat.

"Yessir, it's the same old Brax." Something was missing in Benjy's laughter. "Honey fetch old Brax a glass."

"I'm not particular," said Brax.

"Well I believe I'd like one," Katheryn said.

"One what?" asked Benjy.

"A glass. For the whisky."

Brax popped out of his chair and trotted over to the cupboard to get them. "Well," said Benjy, puzzled, as he poured hers, "this is unusual."

"That's fine right there," she said and drew the glass away.

"Kat don't often partake," Benjy explained.

"Moderation's the secret," she replied.

"Maybe you'd like some water with that, Ma'am?"

"No thank you, Mr. Braxton, I like my whisky straight."

How 'bout your men? Brax wanted to know, and she smiled as though she was reading his mind.

"Well then," Benjy said after he finished pouring the round, "here's to my old pal Brax." He raised his glass high.

"Hear hear!" Brax downed his drink, set the glass on the table and watched Kat take a healthy sip. "Say, Ma'am," he said when the toast was done, "have you any objections to tobacco in your kitchen?"

"Go right ahead." The question surprised her. No one Benjy brought here showed her that courtesy. But John had always inquired before lighting up in another's house. In the silence that followed Brax tapped his pouch for the last flakes and rolled the cigarette carefully. Benjy was pouring whisky down his throat. She turned back to the stranger.

There was a likeness to her late husband, but only on the surface. Was this Brax, underneath, a strong and gentle soul, like John? He certainly didn't look the part of a gentleman. He still dressed like cowboys did right after the war. Anyway he'd surely move on tomorrow and never come back. Yet she was certain if she saw his face five years from today she'd know him.

"Brax is in the cattle business too, ain't that so, Brax?"

"Well, Benjy, I was a fair drover once."

Katheryn finished the drink. It was good. She had enjoyed it and they all could tell. Pleasure lit her face like a lamp; her eyes were diamonds on the desert.

Benjy had seen that look before, plenty of times. But not lately, and again dark clouds began to mass in the skies of his mind. "Want another, Kat?" But she waved the bottle away. "Maybe we'd have more fun if you'd drink with me more," he muttered.

"Señor, Señora." Vicente stood. "I thank you for your hospitality, but we must have come fifty miles today. I apologize if I offend but I am poor company when tired. Is that not so, Señor Brax?"

"Come to think of it, kid, you really ain't such. . ."

He flashed his disarming grin. "So with your permission. . ."

"Of course Vicente," his hostess replied. "Just go right through that door into the hallway. First room on the left is for our guests."

"Got its own washroom and everything," Benjy chimed in.

"Gracias. Please do not trouble yourselves further. Buenas noches."

"It *is* late," Katheryn said when he was gone. She stifled a yawn as she rose. "And alcohol makes me so sleepy." Brax jumped to his feet. He planned on holding her chair out or something but instead just stood awkwardly. Vicente could pull off a gesture like that but to Brax it didn't come easily. "I'm pleased to have met you, Mr. Braxton. Good night." And she disappeared through the doorway.

Katheryn didn't need a lantern to find her way down the hall which split the short east-facing leg of the house. She paused briefly outside the guestroom to hear Vicente clambering into the top bunk, then strode past to the master bedroom at the end of the hallway. She took the coal oil lamp from the night table, lit it, and turned the wick low. The window was open and the air was cool and fresh. She sat on the edge of the big hickory four-poster and stared out into the night at the hulking darkness of the great folded scarps that loomed over the valley to the east.

Brax was interested. Well, she was plenty used to that. What in the world were they doing here anyway? The kid's story about gold was mighty flimsy. Anyone could see they weren't outfitted for prospecting, and it was a long trip to a supplier. Suddenly she had a hunch they would be staying awhile, and with the thought came a fluttery stomach.

Well he *was* attractive. Very much so, in a funny sort of way. That face—somehow it exhibited both strength and helplessness. A little sad-looking, yet the eyes seemed to be grinning at the whole world. They laughed and danced the way Benjy's used to.

Oh, this was horsecrap! Why should this Braxton be any

different from all the other saddle tramps Benjy brought home? Windblown trash, probably rode the outlaw trail. Who the hell else came to Lodgepole anymore? Like all the rest he would pretend to have no past. Such men rarely had a future.

The weak light of the lamp was intrusive. She blew it out and undressed by starlight. It struck her that Brax was old enough to be a veteran. Kat was a toddler back then, and her Ohio home was spared the ravages of the War of the Southern Rebellion, as her father still called it.

A Southerner. A gunslinger. And no doubt flat broke. But those hands, big and callused as they were—would they be as gentle on a woman's body as they'd been rolling that little paper of tobacco? Suddenly she wanted to apologize for trying to steal his horse. The notion of course was comical. Maybe some day they *would* laugh about it. Laugh about it for real, not just with embarrassed little smiles.

Costs nothing to hope, but I can't jump again until I'm sure. And that, like most good-sounding advice, is no help at all. How can a person be sure of *anything,* till it's already gone?


"Well Brax, it's just you and me and that suits me fine." Benjy handed over the bottle.

Brax examined the label. "Pure Tennessee sippin' whisky. You know they're right about it bein' late. I'd like to have a clear head tomorrow, but you sure make it tough, partner. I haven't had whisky like this for. . ."

"What was it Brax, five?"

"Four years, two months."

"Just get out?"

Brax nodded as he drank. "Goddamn, how'd the people who made liquor like this manage to lose the war?" He smacked his lips and wiped his mouth with his sleeve. "You sure got a pretty setup here. Take long to round up a good crew?"

"Well . . ." Benjy drank down three ounces. "Around here help don't come easy. But you know me, Brax, never one to live off a gal's money. So I do jobs in town, you know, chasin' squatters, ridin' fences. Like the old days."

"Weren't no fences in my old days. Gimme some more of that." Benjy handed it over and Brax sipped, reluctant to give the bottle up again.

"Brax, you just wait till you get a look at those quarterhorses."

"So you're wranglin', huh?"

"Oh now and again. We had a contract-buster out here last spring. Learned a lot from the guy. Just a youngster really but damn good with horses. Damn good." His eyes strayed past Brax to the hallway. Vicente entered the room. " 'Bout your age, kid. Sit down. Glad you could make it."

"I thought perhaps a little drink would help me sleep. It has been an exciting evening, eh Señor Brax?"

Brax nodded. "Speaking of horses, Benjy, you lose a couple to rustlers?"

"Nah." He leaned forward on his elbows and lowered his voice. "Bastard won 'em fair and square. If he cheated I couldn't catch him."

"Oh."

"Señor Benjy, would you have a little tobacco?"

Benjy tossed Vicente the pouch. "Well what would you do? Out of cash and sittin' on a full boat, queens high. Trouble is, his was aces high. 'Course, it's no sense to worry Kat with such things so I told her they was run off. And when I seen the fine mounts you boys had, well . . ." He spread his arms, flashed a grin, and sucked another inch from the bottle. "That Kat," he continued, smacking his lips loudly, "that Kat now she is one hell of a gal. Yessir, one *hell* of a gal, if you do get my drift. . ."

"Señor!" Vicente coughed on a lungful of smoke. *"Prudencia!"*

"Whatsamatter don't they do it down there in Old *May-hee-co?* Sure they do, goin' by all them little. . ."

Brax cut it short. "Benjy, I need some shuteye," he said, rising. Benjy grabbed his arm roughly.

"Hey we *did* have some good times, eh buddy? You know, you know I always felt real bad, you drawin' hard time and all, I thought maybe one day I could make it up to you or somethin', you know, and all of a sudden, here we are again."

"Sure, Benjy. Let it be till tomorrow, huh? I don't want to fall asleep here in the kitchen."

"Yeah, O.K., partner, now you sleep in and wake up real hungry, hear? 'Cause Kat's gonna whip you up the best breakfast you ever—"

"Goodnight," said Vicente, already on his way out. Brax followed. "And thanks for the smoke, Señor Benjy," Vicente called from the hall. Benjy took another swallow, stared at the bottle for a moment, and corked it. Then he pulled himself to his feet and headed for the master bedroom.

# Seven

"Don't know what you got against this guy and I don't care. But when you send me on a thousand-mile ride to 'see if he's still alive,' well to me that means be damn sure he ain't." Tores drained the glass and smacked his lips. "Now I admit we didn't handle it too good," he said, pouring himself another brandy from Jordan's bottle, "but goddamn it, Jordan, when you put me up against a man that can better the likes of Keppman, you damn well ought to say something first."

Jordan smashed his fist down onto the desk. "Franklin, there were *three* of you!"

Tores turned his back and walked to the window. "We was tired, had a few drinks," he said evenly. He looked down into the street, then drew the curtains. "That Billy, he just went crazy on the train. Both of 'em, slurpin' whisky and carryin' on like it was the Fourth of July. Tell you the truth I kind of got caught up in it myself."

"You had instructions. You were to try to get him on that train. And failing that I wanted proof of his death. This is the first time you've failed me, Franklin. That's why you've been avoiding me these past days, isn't it?'' Tores was silent. ''Well isn't it?''

Tores spun and faced him. ''You got complaints? Plenty of people lookin' for a guy like me. What with the trouble down in New Mexico over fences and shit.''

Jordan rose. ''Now don't be hasty, Franklin, I need you here.'' He put his hand on the man's shoulder. ''We can't let this guy get away.''

Tores stepped aside letting the hand slide off. *''We?* What's this 'we'? What's this Braxton to me? Who the hell is this guy?''

''Franklin, this is a bad time to start asking questions. You never cared before. Like that last business at Henryville. All you wanted to hear was the land's yours. Well fine, you earned it.''

''You're goddamn right I earned it. Near got killed.''

''They'll be more ranches starting up. The people are coming again. There's talk of Utah becoming a state. You stick with me and I'll take care of you.''

''What do you want from me?''

''Right now I want some thinking. How are we going to find Braxton?''

''You said it yourself.''

''Said what?''

Tores poured another drink. ''Good brandy you got here, Jordan.''

''It's cognac. And take it easy, that's the last of it.''

''You wanna hear what I got in mind or you sendin' me downstairs to buy my own drinks?''

''Speak out.''

''Utah's gonna be a state, well I been hearin' that for years. But the part about the settlers, that's true. And that means the law's comin' back. That means we got to have a sheriff.''

''What are you telling me, Franklin?''

''I'm telling you I'm the new sheriff.''

"You think it's that easy? I'll have to fake records, maybe even hold an election."

"It *is* that easy. A man who can forge deeds can do anything. Give me a badge." He emptied the bottle into his glass and opened the nearest wall cabinet. "It's a way to get Braxton. Keppman, he was my deputy, killed in the line of duty, right? So we put out flyers on the bastard. He committed murder while resisting arrest."

"I told you, Franklin, there's no more cognac."

"You're a liar." Tores held up a fresh bottle. He broke the seal with his thumbnail, pulled the cork with his teeth and poured. "What do you think happens when a *real* lawman comes to Lodgepole? No more crooked games, no more landgrabs."

"Your concern for my welfare is touching."

"We get one of those righteous federal marshalls up here, even you won't pull it off, Jordan. *Especially* you."

"And you could, eh, Franklin?"

"Why not?" He raised the glass to his lips. "There's nothing in my background."

Jordan shook his head. "A sane man would have retired on all the money I've paid out to you."

"Small change, Jordan, small change." He slammed the empty glass down on the desk and headed for the door.

"Two thousand dollars," Jordan said, and Tores spun on his heels. "You heard correctly. Two thousand cash. *If* you bring him in alive. Call that small change?"

"And dead?"

"Half." It might have to be that way. Some things couldn't be helped. It was a fair price. Tores had been a professional long enough. It was easier to bring them in over the saddle than in it. "Go back to Yuma if you have to, start all over again. Get the men you need, I'll pay." Tores opened the door and made to step out. "And I like the idea of wanted posters," Jordan said to his back.

Tores faced him for the last time. "You remember what I

said, Jordan. We let a real sheriff come in here, you're through.''

The door slammed and Jordan stared at the empty space Tores had left behind. He felt as though the room had shrunk. He opened the door, then the window, and the wind promptly turned a neat stack of papers on the desk into a scattered mess on the floor. The gust bore high-country autumn on its breath and Jordan shivered. He slammed the window shut and double-locked the door. Closed spaces were less to be feared than a bullet in the back.

He stopped to retrieve the papers. Titles, deeds, agreements. Harv Jordan was wealthy now and getting richer by the day. The real wealth, he knew, lay in the land itself, not in any gold it might conceal. This was the only useful land among ten million acres of cloud-scraping mountains and parched slickrock desert. The mountain runoff made irrigation possible and hundreds of sections of grassland were tailor-made for livestock. The railroad companies, never slow to sniff out a profit, would soon link the area with every town on the map. And then people would come, and the *real* boom would hit Lodgepole.

Jordan took a map of the area from a drawer and spread it on his desk. He traced the extent of his holdings with a finger and traveled the boundaries in his mind's eye. He crumpled the map in his fist and threw it on the floor. He buried his head in his arms and choked back a sob, then sprung to his feet and paced.

Franklin wasn't the man. To him, Jordan's thoughts and longings were as alien as those of an Australian aborigine. And Ernest was . . . gone. When this damned Braxton thing was over he would rest easier, maybe leave his property with a smart lawyer and return to the civilized world, San Francisco or New York. A knock sounded at the door. ''Who is it?''

''Chang.''

Jordan unlocked the door. A tall slender Oriental stood in

the hallway. He wore a short silk jacket over a floor-length formal gown. His choice of skullcap and carefully prepared queue gave the impression he was dressed for a special occasion.

"Chang, I am glad to see you!" They embraced. "Come in, come in! God, you made good time."

"The train from Salt Lake is very quick, old friend."

"As it ought to be. Your people laid the tracks."

"And yours, Harv, built the road from the station. A longer journey, though a shorter distance, than the train ride from the city."

Jordan eyed the black satchel Chang carried. "Did you bring it?"

"Of course."

"You are an angel sent from heaven!"

Thin lips parted, briefly revealing Chang's stained, decaying teeth. "Not to the men downstairs," he said.

Jordan scowled. "Any trouble? We don't get many Oriental gents in Lodgepole."

Chang shook his head. "No trouble. Just queer looks."

"No words? Surprising."

"Lucky," corrected Chang. "For them." Jordan had to agree. In Salt Lake he had seen Chang kill a man with his bare hands.

"Well, then, let's see it, eh Chang? Open up, open up!"

Chang undid the clasps of the valise and withdrew a pouch of tan goatskin. Jordan accepted the bundle and untied the thongs which drew it together. He reached in and came up with a muddy brown brick. Half a pound of refined opium.

"Sit down, Chang, sit down!" Jordan pointed to his favorite armchair. "Take this one, it's the best." He fussed about pulling over another chair. He slid a small endtable between the two chairs. "Would you like a beverage? Tea? I know you don't drink alcohol."

Chang withdrew a clasp knife from the satchel. "Later, perhaps." Deftly he carved a thumbnail ball from the brick.

"Have you a lamp?" he inquired.

"Yes, yes, everything!" With jerky movements Jordan rummaged in his desk until he found a small glass-bowled apothecary's lamp. "Before I sit," he said as he placed the lamp on the table in front of his guest, "let's get this part of it out of the way, shall we?" He fished into his waistcoat and reeled in a roll of bills. "Your train fare's more than the damn hop," he said jovially.

"Ah, that is not so any more, my friend. There are those in Salt Lake these days who take a dim view of our little pleasure."

"Mormons!" spat Jordan. "I've as much use for Apaches!" He handed over the bills. "The hell with them and their high-minded 'dim view,' eh Chang?" Chang flipped through the bills, rapidly counting. "Take what you need," said Jordan. "I don't argue money with you, Chang."

Chang handed back a small portion of the bankroll. The rest of it disappeared beneath the flowing folds of his garment. Out came a slender pipe as long as his forearm. The stem was of carved teak and morsels of jade and ivory decorated its almond-sized bowl.

"A marvelous pipe, Chang, exquisite. May I?" Jordan lifted it. Lovingly he ran his fingers over the soft fragrant wood and caressed the gem-studded bowl.

Chang acknowledged the compliment with a bow of his head. "It's one of those I made in Canton." He struck a flint and touched the flame to the wick of the lamp. "It has seen half of the world," he added as Jordan gently placed the pipe on the table next to the lamp. With great care Chang adjusted the wick, then impaled the little ball of opium on the end of a long needle and held the drug over the flame. Slowly he cooked the opium into a gummy paste. From time to time he removed it from the flame and by pressing it against the side of the lamp shaped it into an oblong pellet. At last he put this into the bowl of the pipe and tenderly placed the stem in the other man's hands. Jordan leaned forward, held the bowl over the flame of the lamp, and greedily sucked up the sizzling, pungent cloud.

"Chang, I have something for you." Jordan lurched to his feet, tottered part of the way across the room only to collapse with a house-shaking thud. Chang burst into laughter. Grinning, Jordan pulled himself upright and made his unsteady way to the desk where he pulled open a drawer and took out a rolled-up sheet of paper. This he presented to his guest.

Chang unrolled it and held it out at arm's length. It was an ink drawing. "Marvelous!" he gasped. In the picture a Chinese warlord rode an enormous steed. In one hand the warrior held the reins, the other brandished a gleaming scimitar above his head. The horse was wild-eyed with flaring nostrils. The two of them hurtled towards the viewer at a full run. Clouds of dust boiled around them and a vicious cross wind whipped the rider's gowns wildly about. And there was meticulous attention to detail. Embroidered patterns decorated the saddle blankets and dozens of tiny carefully rendered beads adorned the warlord's garments. In the background was the suggestion of impossibly jagged mountains looming over an alien desert studded with exotic plants. The picture was fantastic and frightening and beautiful.

"Why, it bears my face!"

Warmed by his friend's sincere appreciation Jordan smiled but said nothing. Very carefully Chang rolled up the drawing and placed it in the satchel that had held the opium. "This is your work? But of course, who else here knows me? I had no idea you were an artist. This is astonishing, Harv, truly astonishing. You never spoke of it."

"It's something I keep to myself."

"I will cherish this always. It will be framed in the finest laquered bamboo and grace a place of honor in my parlor."

They smoked again. Later they sat on the plush carpet in the gloom of drawn shades, their backs propped up against the wall.

"When do we go to Europe, Chang? In Paris I hear they sit in open-air cafés, because there the summer sun is no enemy. They sit in its warmth and sip absinthe and marvelous cognacs. And there's not so much dust and manure. There's not so many men so quick to do violence. There's not the need. And a man is free to follow his inclinations."

Chang said nothing but his eyes were open. Jordan straightened. "I'm a reasonably wealthy man, Chang. We could leave this wilderness. We could cross the world. A great pilgrimage, to Paris, then overland, to your fabulous, beloved city of Canton—"

"Stop," Chang said firmly. "We'll not make plans. If we are to go it must be at once. In the morning."

"In the morning?"

"It is the last opportunity. I sense that. It is prophecy. It is true."

"There's something—I didn't want to think of this tonight. There is something that must be done first."

"Then I am sorry for you, Harv."

There was a lengthy silence broken by Jordan.

"Chang?"

The response, when it came, was thick and muffled. "Yes?"

"You'll stay here tonight? With me?"

"Of course, old friend. Of course."


Breakfast was everything Benjy had promised and more. The first course was an omelet of green chile and the first bite split Vicente's face into a grin. The eggs were followed by ham hocks and a molasses bread that carried Brax back to the early days of the war, the good days when, as an officer's valet, he had dined in the homes of the wealthiest Southerners. Katheryn's coffee was strong and hot and didn't taste anything like trail dust. Brax held one hand over his distended belly and wave away offers of thirds with the other.

"Ma'am, I can truthfully say that is the best meal I have had in years."

"Why thank you, Mr. Braxton."

"Please. My friends call me Brax."

"My mother, God bless her, she cooked chile heuvos very much like this," said Vicente. "It makes me homesick."

Benjy grinned with pride. "Yessir, Kat sure can cook. Never know it to look at her, but she's one quarter Mex."

"And I am *four* quarters Mex."

It flew past Benjy. "Well then," he said cheerfully. "As I once heard a gentleman say, shall we retire to the sitting room?"

The room took up the lion's share of the main wing. The night before it had been impressive even by starlight, now Brax saw it was larger than many saloons he'd been in and a lot prettier. The fireplace, a stone mason's masterpiece, was nearly big enough to walk into. Overhead giant rafters of seasoned Douglas fir gave the place a look of timeless strength. A floor-to-ceiling bookcase of rich dark oak hid the east wall. Brax figured the kid could lose himself for months among those volumes.

In this room the feminine touch was not in evidence. Everything was in browns, ochres, and mahoganies. A gun rack displayed Kentucky long rifle, a scattergun, several military carbines, and an old Sharps buffalo gun. The head of a mountain sheep, a snow-white ram with a magnificent set of horns, graced the mantel and trophies of other successful hunts—the heads of pronghorn, a black bear, and a cougar—decorated the walls. What impressed Brax most was the south window. It was at least five feet wide and three feet high, and of double-strength glass. The three men sank into oversized wicker chairs facing the window. The view stretched past the small dusty front yard, over the rolling grassy range to the scrubby foothills on the horizon. Benjy leaned back and put his feet on the plank table of varnished spruce. "Not bad, eh?" he said with a sweeping gesture that

included the house and the land. Abruptly he rose and sauntered over to a cabinet. "How 'bout a little eye-opener,
boys?"

"Too early for me, partner." Brax held up his cup. "Still
got my java here. Like to get the old brain working again
before I start shuttin' it down."

"How 'bout you, kid? Just to show there's no hard feelin's
left over."

"No thank you. And you need not concern yourself with
hard feelings, Señor Benjy."

"Suit yourself. You're all right, kid. Don't let me get your
goat, know what I mean?" He took a drink from the bottle, a
big drink, and smacked his lips. "Real nice, livin' in these
parts, Brax. Nice weather, too. Invigoratin' winters, like
North Texas, only not near as windy. And the summers, they
ain't nothin' like those hellholes down in Arizona." He had
drained four or five ounces and his eyes were shining.

"Say Benjy, you always drink like that?"

"Like what, Brax?" He placed the bottle on the table.
"Hell, buddy, this here's a special occasion if ever there was
one. Brax is back!" He leaned across the table and spoke
softly. "Say, hard time, Yuma, huh? Guess I was just the
lucky one is all. Heard for sure you was dead, you know."

"So you said. Who'd you hear this from?"

"Well, story goes you was in a break, bunch of guys took
down a guard and headed out the front gate, but I didn't
believe it. I know you, Brax, and a man's got to be stupid, or
plain nuts, to go up against a Gatling gun."

Brax stole a glance at Vicente, saw that look of concentra-
tion in his face. But Vicente said nothing. "Who told you
this, Benjy?"

Benjy raised the bottle to his lips. "You sure you won't
join me?" They shook their heads. He took a smaller drink
and set the bottle down again. "Let's see. Think it was Billy,
sure, it was Billy. You remember Billy Ferson, right?"

"I remember Billy Ferson."

"He thought it was you, he was sure you was one of the

fellows bought it during the bust-out.''

"That cuss is so mixed up, he wouldn't know for sure if *he* was killed during a bust-out.''

Benjy's laughter filled the big room. "Probably so, Brax, probably so. He sure is one dumb critter.'' He took another drink. "He's in Lodgepole now, you know.''

Vicente spoke. "Are there others in Lodgepole who were in Yuma Prison?''

"Not that I can recall. Let's see. Well, once old Billy was in his cups and he told me, guess it's a secret or something, said Mr. Jordan did a stretch there too.''

Brax's cup slipped to the floor as if the fingers around the handle had died, and, as a storm-driven ocean smashes a canoe, it all came back. The rainstorm, a cold desert soaker, the worst kind; the dank rock tunnel he had chipped out of the hill with his own hands; the hacking glazed-eyed Indian and that monster of a man. The pictures weren't as awful as the feelings that ushered them in, the worst of it was the helpless rage. And all the while the soggy wind danced around the high mud-brick walls and mocked the damned souls inside. The shudder rocked his shoulders.

With an effort he bent to gather the pieces of the shattered cup but Vicente was already there mopping the spill with his handkerchief. "Never mind, Señor Brax.'' Vicente turned to Benjy. "Please go on.''

"Benjy,'' Brax said in what he felt was a calm voice, "are you talking about Harv Jordan, a very big man with a scarred face?''

Benjy nodded. "Not only big but a big wheel in these parts.'' For a moment his bubbly manner sagged. "Bought up mortgages when the bank pulled out.'' His eyes drifted to the bottle on the table. "Loans money, holds markers on places.''

Vicente still held the pieces of the broken cup. "Is there a man in Lodgepole, a stupid-looking, stout young man with several missing teeth?''

Benjy's smile returned. "Sounds like Billy to me.''

"And another," Vicente continued, "he has tiny eyes, a hard face as if chiseled from stone. He wears two pistols and speaks softly, like a woman."

Benjy knitted his brow as he sorted faces. "Why yeah!" he said at last, slamming his fist into his palm. "Tores! Frank Tores, sure. Yeah, Tores is all right. Good man to drink with. Ought to hear him badmouth Jordan, real funny! Lucky poker player too. Too damn lucky." He drained his glass. "Never was in Territorial, though. Not to my knowledge. Why, what's up?"

"Oh, a friend of mine in Chihuahua, he described some men he once met there. Wanted me to ask after them. They are well, no?"

Benjy's head bobbed. "Oh sure, they're just fine."

"And there was one more gentleman, a good dresser, with sun-colored hair."

"That'd be Ernie Keppman." He shook his head. "Won't find him though. Drunken redskin got him in Arizona, just a little while ago."

Vicente's face dropped convincingly. "Ah, but my friend will be sorry to hear that. He said these three were a lot of fun."

"And he's right. Damned shame. I always say, you won't tame the Injuns by puttin' 'em on reservations. Just seems to make 'em madder."

Brax reached out and put his hand on Benjy's shoulder. "Benjy, don't tell anyone we're here."

"Brax, you on the run again? You sure come to the right place."

"Well you never can tell, so just don't fail me, hear?"

"You know me, Brax. Never one to mess in another man's affairs." He winked. " 'Specially if there's no money in it."

# Eight

"Ferson and Tores, of course, must die."

"Of course," said Brax, studying the young Mexican's face. Unbroken quarterhorses milled about in their pen while in nearby pasture a Morgan dam and her yearling grazed. Brax leaned against the rails of the corral, lulled by the rustle of the leaves and the groan of the windmill pump. His eyes roamed the peaceful valley.

Up close the ranch had the look of neglect. Fences sagged, the barn leaked. A hundred yards away a gently sloping, south-facing acre lay fallow; Brax guessed it had once been a vegetable garden. This place should be alive with the sounds of harvesting and haying and the shouts of hired hands. The smell of cut legume and steaming preserves should be in the air. In high-country winter didn't wait for a calling card. This morning high thin clouds painted the sky a sad gray and the land bathed in the color of slate. Only last week the delicate green of the quaking aspen had spangled in the breeze and the sunlight. Now they hurled their challenge in the face of the coming season with dazzling displays of gold and orange.

"Tell me about Harv Jordan, Señor Brax."

Gusts raked the mountain spine that split the Territory, a north wind that dared them to keep their hats on. Brax faced his friend, and for just a moment Vicente felt the cold blast could have come from this man's heart. "You don't miss much, do you?" was all Brax said.

"A man would have been dead in his cups to miss your reaction when the name was spoken, Señor Brax."

"Do me a favor, will you? I quit calling you keed and you quit calling me Señor goddam Brax, huh?" As he said this his fists were clenched at his sides and he seemed smaller somehow, as if his body had coiled in on itself. But his face had neither colored nor whitened, and his eyes did not shine with anger. Rather they looked as if they had lost their life, been drained, and replaced with something else, something beyond rage. Something closer to fear, maybe, but Vicente sensed it was not the fear of any foe that could be met in battle.

Whatever it was Brax had revealed shamed him; this was obvious in the way he hastily turned his back. He bent his knees and pretended to examine the lower rails of the corral fence. "We'd best quit this jawbeatin' and get to work," he muttered. "Wonder where he keeps his tools. Didn't see any in the barn."

Vicente felt the moment slipping and had to press it or lose it. Quietly he asked, "Is Harv Jordan the kind of man who pays others to do his killing?"

Brax straightened and again took up his position against the rails facing the far sweep of the valley.

"Leave it be, Vicente."

Vicente's reply was a silent and nearly imperceptible nod. Brax pushed himself off the fence and swiveled a half turn to the right. He pointed to an inconspicuous clapboard shed just the other side of the ranch house. "Looks as good a place as any to keep hammer and nails." Vicente grunted and started off across the front yard to the shed. Since he didn't know if he expected Brax to come along he wasn't surprised to find himself walking alone.


Benjy was a trifle unsteady on his feet as he wobbled into the kitchen. His eyes were red-rimmed and his voice gravelly. He plopped down at the table and rubbed his temples. "Where's Brax?" he wanted to know, and it came out as a croak.

"Outside working," Kat said without looking at him. "Remember that?"

"Remember what?"

"Work. Remember work?" She stopped wiping the counter and tossed the rag into the basin where it plopped soddenly and spilled gray greasy dishwater onto the floor. She untied her apron and hung it on a peg on her way to the door.

"Where you goin'?" he rasped.

She stopped. "They'll be wanting to fix the barn. I thought they could use a hand. What with you having another head-full this morning."

"You'd do best to stay here." His voice carried and the tone was not pleasant. To Vicente, who was passing the open window at that moment, the sounds coming from the kitchen were arresting. He crouched below the window and settled in to listen.

"You never used to throw orders around," she was saying. "And I'm not about to let you start now."

"Well, they don't need your help." Benjy was backing off some. "They's earnin' their keep so they don't need your help. Nobody works for free here."

She brightened, then caught herself. "You fixing to hire them on?" She hoped she'd wrung the anticipation from her voice.

"You'd like that, huh?" he taunted. With some effort he pulled himself up out of his chair and lurched across the room to her. He brought his face uncomfortably close. "I said you'd like that, wouldn't you?"

She took two steps back. "I heard you and, yes, I would like that. Lord knows we need help around here."

"Sure. I know the kind of help you mean." He started to circle the room with long strides, head down. "He's looking good to you, ain't he? Yeah . . ." His head bobbed like a barrel in whitewater. "I believe he is at that. Also strong and reliable, like someone who could take charge."

"Whatever are you talking about?"

Benjy seemed not to have heard. "Reliable, responsible, sober. That's it, ain't it?" He stood in place and fished a fat Cuban cigar out of his shirt pocket.

"When did you start buying those?" she asked.

"What, I don't deserve a decent smoke now and again?" he said, pulling a strike-anywhere from the pocket of his Levis. He shook his head. "Here it comes again. The squawk about money."

"No, I was—"

"It just so happens I didn't buy it. Harv Jordan give it to me."

"Mr. Jordan? The saloonkeeper?" Benjy didn't miss the look of alarm that flashed across her face. "Benjy, I've heard awful things about that man. You'd do well to stay away."

"So now you pick my friends, is that it?" He was shouting. Savagely he struck his match across the kitchen table. It burst into flame leaving an ugly dark streak in its wake.

She eyed the damaged table top. "You're a bastard," she said evenly. "Get yourself and that stinking stick out of my kitchen. This talk is done."

Benjy fired up his cigar, snuffed the match with his fingers and dropped it where he stood. "So you don't think Brax would take your money, huh?"

"My God, are you still runnin' on about him? I don't even know the man! He's just another cowboy drifter from Texas, or wherever the hell they all come from."

"Hell and Texas, honey, it's the same damn thing." He puffed mightily on the Havana and a massive cloud of bitter gray smoke rolled forth.

"I told you, get that thing out of here. Hand-rolls are one thing, but not those damn cee-gars! And I don't want *you* in here either. Go out and help your Texas drifter, or go stick your damn head in a horse trough, it might cure your hangover, but just leave me alone!"

Outside the window Vicente squatted, chin in cupped hand. Silently he shifted his cramping knees. It was unmanly to skulk in the shadows, eavesdropping, but it was imperative that he learn as much as possible about this place and these people.

Benjy sank into a chair and stared at his feet. "I bet you think Brax could turn this place around, show a profit," he muttered. "And keep you in finery."

"Benjy, when did I ever give a good goddamn about finery?"

"Lemme tell you something, Kat." He looked up at her, his voice rising. "Brax and me is one of a kind. Absolutely, we are one of a kind."

"Oh there's no kind like you!" Now she was yelling. "How many men would toss this all away? What were you when you came here, tell me that! A lost saddle tramp who couldn't dig up four bits to share a bed over the saloon!"

"Now you cut that this minute! I will not listen to this 'I took you out of the gutter' shit!"

"But it's not shit," she said sadly. "It's true."

"Maybe so," he admitted after a pause. "But to that tune I don't sing along."

She took a tentative step towards him. "Benjy, tell me this please, why, Benjy, *why?*" She spread her hands. "Why? Why the drinking? Most men drink, I don't begrudge a man his whisky, but each day, a bottle, more?" She laid her hands on his shoulders and rocked him gently as she stood over him. "Why?"

There was no answer. Her arms went limp and she dropped her hands to her sides. Finally he spoke. "It makes things easier to take," he said almost inaudibly.

"Things? What things?"

"Things. The things I do when I go away." He reached for her. "Kat, I had enough. Let's quit this needlin' each other."

She took a step back, waiting for more, but this was all she was going to get out of him. "Whatever your trouble is, you don't seem to be trying to get out of it." She shook her head sadly. "You're a simple man, Benjy. You only see the simple side to a problem. Need money? Go work for the thieves. Feel bad about it later? Drink. That way you don't feel at all. Do you, do you really think you can have it both ways? Our life here and whatever it is you do with those outlaws in Lodgepole?" Her glance fell on the dishrag on the floor by the basin and she stooped to pick it up.

Benjy pouted. "Those 'outlaws,' like you call 'em . . . well it brings in a little cash, don't it? You don't shirk from spendin' it." He slammed his fist down on the table. "Hell, I could drown in a barrel of bourbon and you'd cheer if there was money in it."

"Benjy, listen to me. It wasn't like this last year, remember? And we had a love life. Remember how it used to be? Not very long ago, was it? You think on that." She looked down and was surprised to see she held the soiled, dripping dishrag in hands. "Aw hell! For a moment you never mind about me, think of this place. It's a good ranch. This is prime land, you've said it yourself a dozen times. What I can't see is, you're always going on about how much you love this spread only there's never the time or the energy to do anything for it."

"But if *he* could take over, he'd do it right, is that it?"

"I'm not talking about *him*." She flung the filthy rag into his face.

Outside Vicente heard the rough scrape of a chair and the dull crash as it toppled and hit the floor. He sprang to the door and rapped loudly upon it. Immediately the door was thrown back. The hinges squawked and the door banged against the jamb. Benjy stood blocking the opening, filling the space.

Vicente tried his respectful smile. "Excuse me, Señor Benjy, I—"

"Been soakin' up every goddam word, you sneakin' greaser bastard!" Benjy swung with a half-open fist, caught him on the cheek and knocked him out of the doorway. Vicente's knife was out so fast they saw only the flash of a sunbeam striking the steel. He crouched, a cornered animal ready to spring, eyes wide, muscles corded.

"No!" Katheryn screamed, rushing across the room to them. "Put it away, for God's sake, put it away!" Benjy was backing off, hands spread and held high.

Vicente saw the pleading in her eyes, saw the terrified Benjy cringing, still backing across the room, and his fury left him like air from a punctured balloon. "Yes," he said. Slowly he sheathed the knife, though a tremor still ran through his hands. As his muscles relaxed he seemed to deflate. "I have lost my head." He rubbed his reddened cheek which was only now beginning to smart. "It is dangerous to lose one's head," he said, and for a moment the grin was back. But only for a moment. His eyes sought Benjy's. "Dangerous for me and dangerous for you." Benjy could not meet his gaze but grimaced and turned away. "Ah," Vicente continued airily, "I suppose one should not be so quick to skewer his host, eh? Bad manners, as Señor Brax would say. So now I must ride on."

He was turned and halfway back out the door when Kat stopped him. "Vicente! You are *my* guest. You must not leave until Mr. Braxton is ready. You're partners, right? It would be a very bad thing to split up on our account. So you may not leave without him, or you offend me greatly."

Vicente faced them again and sighed. "Very well, Señora. But I must tell your *meester* Benjy here, if ever he lays hand on me again, this blade shall be the end of him." He turned stiffly and closed the door behind him.

"My God, Kat, he's awful quick with that thing!"

"Not a good one to rile, Benjy."

"No," Benjy agreed. "Not a good one at all."


Brax was exactly as he had left him. "Not in there either?" he called as soon as Vicente was within earshot. Vicente stopped, puzzled, then remembered his purpose.

"I forgot to look for the tools, Señor Brax."

"You forgot? Between here and the shed, you forgot?" He shook his head. "Jesus, you were gone long enough. Where'd you go off to?"

Vicente did not reply. Instead he nodded in the direction of the barn. The barn door was sliding open with a moan. Out of the gloom stepped Benjy Thomas with a magnificent pinto stallion in tow. Straining, he shouldered the door close. He hoisted himself into the saddle and shook the reins once. The great horse moved towards them at an easy lope.

The beast stood nearly seventeen hands, a jet-black beauty with snow-white stockings and large white blotches on its chest and shoulders. Like parts of a great engine the muscles rose and fell under its finely curried coat. Brax pictured it at a full run, those muscles surging, the uncropped mane flying stiff like a banner in the wind.

With an easy familiar motion Benjy teased the reins and the animal stopped almost in mid-stride. Finally the two men at the corral wrested their eyes from the striking mount to the rider now towering above them. No wide grin awaited them. Only eyes that were narrow and bloodshot and a face that was unreadable. "Goin' to town on business," he announced and scratched the stubble on his chin.

"Plenty of fence mendin' to be done around here," Brax said conversationally.

The man on the big horse pulled at the corners of his mouth, then leaned back in his saddle. With exaggerated care he surveyed his domain. "Don't see no stock loose that oughtn't to be," he said.

"A little work now save a lot later." Benjy shrugged and raised the reins. "And I'd like to earn that meal," Brax added.

"Suit yourself. Want vittles, ask Kat." He brought the steed around, touched his spurs to its flanks and the big paint surged into a canter. Brax and Vicente watched Benjy's velvet hat bounce up and down above his dust. The hat shrank and vanished as the heavy hoofbeats faded and the sounds of the day returned.

They looked at once another. "Hangover?" Vicente suggested innocently.

"Somethin's on his mind." Brax fingered a broken fence rail. "Shit, we didn't ask him where the damn tools are," Brax took a step towards the shed. Vicente stretched out his arm and stopped him.

"Señor Brax . . ." He was determined to get an answer.

Brax sighed. "All right, what?"

"Is Jordan a man who pays others to do his killing?"

This time Brax removed his Stetson and slapped it against his thigh, raising a cloud of red grit. "Yep," he said.

"Obviously you do not wish to discuss this."

"Obviously."

"And I do not pry. But if Jordan did send those men it is right that you have the privilege of killing him yourself."

Brax studied his friend's eyes. "You're mighty casual about killin', boy."

"A real man does not philosophize about a job that must be done. He simply does it."

"Oh? Is that so? How many, Vicente? How many notches you cut in your what—nineteen, twenty years?"

"Many, Señor Brax," he said huffily. "Outlaws, renegade Mescaleros, many!"

"Horsecrap. A man with as much schooling as you don't have much time for killing. No, hear me out, I'm not saying you're no dude. Hell man, you read sign with the best I've seen. You're sure no slouch with that rifle and I'll wager you know a thing or two about that blade you carry. But you ain't no big bad killer. Not yet, anyway.''

"Two," Vicente said quietly.

"Two?"

"They were beasts, Señor Brax! Savage beasts, that would rob and kill a gentle old man!''

"Take it easy kid, you're agitated." Brax waited. Then: "Tell me something if you can," he said gently. "How did it feel? When you killed these two men, how did you feel?''

"Awful," said Vicente. "It was awful.''

"I see.''

"But it had to be done, Señor Brax, it had to be done.''

"If you say so, kid. I wasn't there.''

"It was Rosa's padre, Brax, they cut off his fingers for the rings, they shot him many times and left him to die in a ditch. . .''

Sadly Brax shook his head. "I seen it often, kid. The finest man, sometimes the finest man just seems to have the knack, he draws death like shit draws flies. Don't you become like that, kid. I can't tell you how, but just don't.''

"I have had to defend my village against plundering Indians and evil pistoleros, I have fired on men but never was I sure it was my bullet that felled them. Until, until those two who murdered Señor Felix. And still, still I would not change it if I could. I ask you, Señor Brax, these men we now seek, are they not of the same breed? They shoot a young girl, they would have killed you even as you slept! Señor Brax, I say to you, to kill is often necessary.''

"Necessary? Sure it's necessary. For three years I killed, three bloody bastard years sogging through the swamps and killing. I was younger than you, kid. I killed in a hundred places—Pea Ridge, Lookout, Vicksburg. But for what? For what? Honor? States' rights? I didn't even know what the words meant!''

Brax searched for cigarette makings but came up empty. "The South, the South was like the Indians. Doomed. Just a matter of time now before the last warrior's penned up, in them big jails they call reservations. Ah, gimme a smoke." Vicente pulled out a fresh pouch and Brax remembered they had finished the last of their tobacco last night. "Where?"

"Señora Katheryn give it to me. To give to you." Vicente rolled two fat smokes and waited for him to continue.

"I'm not much on preaching, but let me tell you a story. Maybe you'll think before getting into something you can't handle. After the war I just drifted with the herds. Riding from Texas to Kansas and drawing pay for it, that was my notion of a good deal. Then someone back East dreams up barbed wire, and all or a sudden it's everywhere. Like that." He snapped his fingers. "The days of the big drives are finished.

"Well, I never could shake the feeling things were better beyond those flats, or on the other side of that mountain." He accepted the smoke and a light. "Thanks. So I kept moving. Only now it seems a man's got to stay put to earn an honest living. And I start seeing things I can't fathom. Like I see folks getting rich, they don't work for this money, they just sign their name twice—once when they get a piece of land and again when they sell it. Plain to any fool the land was never theirs to begin with."

"You turned outlaw."

"Title office. Clerk pulled a gun, I had to shoot. I'm no churchgoer but I still thank the Lord that man didn't die. He was just a poor fool who thought he was doin' his duty."

"That's why you went to prison."

Brax nodded. "A lousy three hundred bucks. The Law showed, Benjy panicked and skeedaddled. I went back for the money. Got two to five instead."

Vicente coughed. "Prison Hill," he said, "it is not a nice place."

Brax's eyes were glued to the far wall of mountains against

the northern sky. To the right one lone peak lost its top among the clouds. Brax stared at the scar in its flank that was Lodgepole. Only his lips moved.

"I seen men bustin' rocks in the sun till their minds broke. When a man falls apart in Territorial he goes to the crazy hole, a hole cut out of solid rock, hardly room to stand or turn around. I seen Indians dropping like flies of the consumption, they were warriors once. Man breaks the rules or tries a bust-out, it's the snake den. Dungeon where you stand alone, chained to the wall, in the dark you hear things scuttle and slither all around you. Come out with welts from the scorpions, like a flogging. The poison burns for days.

"No, kid, Prison Hill is not a nice place." He accepted another hand-rolled. Vicente struck a light off the fencepost. "Know what they did with all them rock chips we busted up? Sold 'em to the townsfolk, they needed stone to mix with their adobe. The virtuous citizens and their bargain-price rock chips. They built their churches out of them."

Vicente let out his breath. "You have a way with words, Señor Brax."

Brax faced him and Vicente was glad to see he was almost back; his eyes nearly smiled again. "Didn't mean to go on like that, kid, it's just that in a place like that, even a man like me isn't safe. Ah, I can't explain that, but what I'm trying to say, what I meant to say before I got started on this, see, unless you're already inside, something happens to you when you're around death. Something spoils, like meat in the sun."

The leaves rustled and the windmind groaned. Somewhere over the hill an unseen steer lowed. "I must avenge the death of my betrothed," Vicente said. "It is the way."

Brax whipped off his Stetson and threw it to the ground. *"The way!* You think this was just a sad story about my rough life, huh? There's no goddamn barbed wire fence separatin' right and wrong, and Rosa was no soiled dove or any of that crap!"

Vicente took a deep breath. "Señor Brax, I must ask that you withdraw those remarks."

"Or what? Or you'll *kill* me?"

"Señor. . ."

" 'Avenge the death of my betrothed'!" he spat. "She plied a rough trade in a hardcase town and her luck ran out. All there is to it. While you read books and practiced shooting birds!"

"Señor, I demand satisfaction!"

"*You demand satisfaction?* You greasy little bastard, first you try to gun me down, now you demand satisfaction!" Brax lunged for him but Vicente sidestepped, and he fell face-first into the dust. Brax scrambled to his feet and un-buckled his gunbelt. "You drop your iron and get rid of that pigsticker and we'll see about satisfaction!"

Vicente yanked out his knife and hurled it at the far fence rails where it buried itself halfway to the hilt. "You, my friend, are sorely in need of a lesson in manners!"

"Fellows!" A gentle wind carried Katheryn's voice. "Lunch is on," she called innocently. They turned and looked at her, framed by the kitchen window. "Come and get it while it's good and hot!"

Brax lowered his hands to dust himself off. He tried to smile. "Kid, fightin' one another really seems like the last goddamn thing we need."

"Si. You are right. You must not feel that your words are in vain, Señor Brax. My feelings often crowd my thoughts." He extended his hand.

"And I, well, I get kind of wound up, thinking about Yuma and all . . ." His words trailed off as they shook. "We'll see 'bout fixing this place up some after lunch, huh?" They started for the house.

"Señor Brax, may I say one more thing? I know a man who hunts game only when he is hungry. He kills to live. Is it not the same, to hunt a man to keep him from killing us?"

"Well, sure, kid but runnin' a man down, that never was

my style. Seen rustlers tracked and shot on sight, or hung. No time for a trial, right? Seen the same thing with Indians, plenty of times. Always makes my stomach kick over.''

Vicente had to smile. ''And do you think everyone in the West loves Mexican Nationals, Señor Brax?''

Benjy Thomas rode his pinto up the main street of Lodgepole, past the boarded-up shops and taverns, the one operating livery and the surviving supply store. He hitched the horse to the rail in front of Harv's Emporium, walked in and downed two shots. He took a deep breath, as if sucking in his nerve, and strode up the curved staircase to stop before the door to Jordan's suite. Before he could knock the door opened and an Oriental stepped out. Chang did not close the door behind him or look at Benjy. Benjy watched him walk down the hall the opposite way and disappear. Puzzled, he reached into the room and knocked softly on the open door.

''What now?'' The voice was muffled, though no door stood between them.

''Benjamin Thomas. Like to speak with you, Mr. Jordan.''

Jordan wanted no more visitors this afternoon. He was listless and his head was throbbing. He knew the feeling all too well. There was too much at stake to continue the binge, but if he didn't take more he would feel lousy the rest of the day. And for Jordan the day had just started.

''All right, Thomas, but be quick about it.'' Benjy stepped in. ''Close the goddamn door. And don't slam it, for Christ's sake!'' Benjy removed his tan velvet hat, and stood before the desk fingering the brim. Jordan leaned back in his chair. ''Just get to the point, O.K.?''

''All right, Mr. Jordan, I will.'' He pointed to the safe behind the desk. ''You keep the title to the Harris ranch in there, don't you?''

''You come to pay off?''

"Maybe. I got something that could be of great interest to you."

"Oh?" Jordan pointed to the decanter on a cabinet shelf. "I forget my manners, Benjamin. I've heard you're a drinking man. That's cognac, not brandy."

"Why that's right kind of you, Mr. Jordan." Benjy headed gratefully for the shelf.

"Now, what is it you want to tell me?"

"Well, Mr. Jordan." He filled a glass to the brim and drained half of it with one gulp. "How much might it be worth to you?"

"What am I supposed to do, bid blind? How can I price something if I don't know what it is? And don't drink like that, goddamn it, take small swallows or none at all, hear me?"

"Sorry, Mr. Jordan, but it sure is good."

"You always were a man of taste if not couth. I can tell that from your woman. Now, speak up or get out. What have you got?"

Benjy was many things but he was no fool. Take Vicente's interest in Jordan's three top gunmen, one of whom had just died in Arizona under strange circumstances. Add Brax's reaction to Jordan's name, and Brax wanting their presence kept a secret. It all added up to something. Benjy didn't know what but this was no time to be testing the water with his toes. It was time to jump right in.

"Don Braxton."

Benjy fancied he could read faces like other men read maps, and he was sure it was more than a flicker of interest which crossed the face before him.

"What makes you think that name means anything to me?" It amazed Jordan the way his lingering narcotic haze had instantly vanished. "Would you be so kind as to pour me a drink, Mr. Thomas? Fill the snifter one third of the way, please."

Benjy went for broke. "One thousand cash and you tear up the marker."

"And in return for this considerable investment I get . . ."

"Braxton. Any way you want him. I know where he is and he trusts me."

Jordan rose, stepped to the office safe and worked the combination with a steady, practiced hand. He withdrew a pile of papers, dumped them on the desk top and rummaged until he found the right one. "You are talking quite a bit of money, friend," he said, studying the document.

"And you're talking a lot of man. If Brax don't want to be found, he just ain't going to be found."

"What makes you think I want him that badly?"

"Call it arithmetic. Add this, add that. Call it a hunch. But you want him, Mr. Jordan."

"Have you been talking to Billy? Franklin?"

"I've been talking to Braxton."

"Hmm, I really must stay on top of my affairs. According to these papers I'll soon have legal right to foreclose."

"What do you need with legal rights when you got Tores's gun?"

Jordan glared. "I don't let many men talk to me that way, Thomas, but you do have a point. What makes you think I can't force you to tell me?"

"I don't think you could. 'Sides," he added a hastily improvised lie, "if I don't meet him tonight he will take steps to protect himself."

"You've actually seen him? He's here, in Lodgepole?"

"Look, Mr. Jordan, what's a few thousand to you? It means everything to me."

"I don't like shakedowns, Thomas, but I will go you one better. Give me Braxton and I'll foreclose. Then I'll just sign the deed over to you." Jordan could see he'd struck a nerve. "Everyone knows it's just a matter of time before they send a marshall in here. I can't doublecross you because it will be all legal. Here, I'll sign my part now."

If Benjy had legal title to the land Kat couldn't send him away. And she would never leave the ranch.

"I like that idea, Mr. Jordan. I like it real well. But I'll need cash too. I'll need the thousand."

"Compromise. Five hundred. It'll be in your pocket when you walk out of here. You sign the deed when I've got Braxton."

Benjy stuck out his hand. "Mr. Jordan, you've got yourself a deal."

# Nine

His eyes grew like a child's in a candy store. "Deer meat!" Brax shouted.

"And grits," Katheryn announced, serving them up.

"It has been some time," said Vicente. "We did not shoot any deer on the trail."

Brax gestured with his fork. His mouth was full and some of his words got swallowed. "Delicious," he managed. "And it sure is a lovely place you folks have here, Ma'am."

"Kat. Please call me Kat."

"It *is* fabulous, Señora Kat," Vicente offered. "It is in need of a little work, though."

"Yes, Vicente," she said evenly. "I know." She took her place at the table. The empty fourth chair, just a little higher than the rest, seemed to loom over them. Kat did not take a plate. She just stared out the window.

At last Brax said, "Aren't you going to join us, Kat?"

She liked the sound of it from him and favored him with a flash of a smile. But she didn't look at them directly. "I'm not hungry now, thank you."

"Good grits, huh kid?" Brax said lamely, and Vicente nodded enthusiastically.

Katheryn's chair screeched against the floor as she abruptly turned to face them. "What brings you to these parts, Mr. Braxton?"

Her question took him by surprise. "Lookin' to buy some stock," he heard himself say.

"Oh? Then you're knowledgeable about cattle?"

"Uh . . . some. Drove the ornery beasts for a number of years. Texas, Kansas, Colorado. . ."

Vicente pushed his chair back from the table. "I know little of cattle but I have patched many holes and fixed many fences."

"Hey you're not done eatin' already, kid?"

"Si. And it was superb." He rose, sensing with certainty that she wanted to be alone with Brax. "So with your kind permission, Señora, I attend to this mending." Before you could reply the door banged shut. The room seemed smaller and closer without him.

Brax cleared his throat. The sound of it was embarrassingly loud. "Well . . ." he faltered. Through the window he could see Vicente enter the storage shed. "Sure is pretty here." Vicente emerged carrying two hammers and a bucket Brax assumed contained nails.

"It is," she said. The way she was looking at him now, so directly, made him uncomfortable.

"It sort of reminds me, this spread here, of a little place I worked one year on the lower Pecos. Only instead of all these cedar trees we had oak."

She gulped her coffee cup dry and set it down on the table a little harder than she meant to. "You know, it's not widely known, but there's quite a bit of good grazing land here. Only we're sort of surrounded by the desert."

Brax nodded. "The Slickrock. I've seen some mean country but not quite like this. Land goes up and down instead of out and about. A million canyons and each one chock-full of boulders and spires and rock bridges leading nowhere."

"More coffee?"

"No thank you. Too much java makes me jumpy."

"Think I will." And she got up to pour herself another cup. "It is beautiful, though," she said from the stove. Her view out the window included Vicente at the far corral. Briefly she watched as he mouthed curses and shook the sting out of the hand he'd smacked with the hammer. She turned back to her guest. "I mean even the desert. In a funny way. Not beautiful like pasture country or green mountains, of course, but beautiful in its own way. Different. Magnificent. Kind of makes a person feel small, makes him want to look inside himself. That make any sense to you?"

"I think I know what you're trying to say. The part about looking inside yourself. I figure maybe that's one reason so many folks hate the desert. Don't like what it does to 'em."

"But not the Indians," she said and sat down opposite him.

"You're right about that. To them it's home. No, it's more than that even. I've wondered about that, how they seem to feel the land is alive, and how some places are magical."

"There's nothing like this where I grew up."

"Oh? And where was that?"

"Virginia," she said. She lifted her coffee and drank. Her eyes were wide and coquettish as they peered at him over the bottom of the cup. "And you?"

"Nebraska Territory."

She couldn't help it. She put her cup down and looked straight at him. "Forgive me for saying so, Mr. Braxton, but you're a poor liar."

Brax grinned right back at her. "And so are you," he said.

"I am that," she laughed. "But I hope I'm a better liar than you. You've got Texas all over you like it was branded on your face."

"Maybe it is. Texas is like that. And you—let's see, before you crossed the Divide I'd wager the farthest south you'd been was the middle of Indiana."

"Close. Ohio. I feel silly, don't you?"

"Uh huh. Sometimes I just plain forget, how long it's been since that goddamn war."

"I was too young to understand about the war."

"I was too. But I went anyway."

"I figured as much. I don't know why but I did."

"I suppose my head got all filled up with the honor of Texas and such junk."

There was kindness in her smile. She was enjoying their small talk but there wasn't much time left and there might be few other chances to be alone with him. He was staring out the window again, no doubt waiting for her to pick up the conversation. But she had to beat back that hollow feeling in her stomach and take a deep breath before she began.

"Mr. Braxton. . ."

He faced her. "I believe you know me well enough to call me Brax."

"Maybe." That smile flickered again. "But I think I like Don better." Then she leaned over the table. The drawstrings of her calico homespun came undone and Brax's eyes, like a schoolboy's, were pulled into the cleft of her plump breasts. He realized then how plainly he was staring and abruptly turned away.

She leaned back and tied the strings with a business-like motion. Were they left loose on purpose? She was no swooner or Sunday-school hypocrite. She went on as if nothing had happened. And, Brax realized, nothing had.

"What I was going to say, Don, was Benjy told me about you."

Brax jerked upright in his chair. "He did?"

"Oh I'm sure he doesn't recall. It was about a year ago. I only remembered it this morning, but, I mean, how many people are called Brax?"

"What'd he say?"

"He was in one of his sentimental moods, he was drinking that night. He didn't drink much then. Anyway, he started talking about his boyhood friends and he worked his way up through the war and after. Let's see, that's when you met, right? Right after the war?'' Brax nodded. ''Then I remember it right. Benjy said you were the best friend a man could ask for. That he could trust you with his life.''

Brax grunted. ''It's true we were close once. As you see, we went our separate ways.''

''Well . . .'' There was a long pause as she hunted for the best way to say it. ''Well, what I really mean to say is, I mean if Benjy trusted you maybe I can too. Oh hell, I might as well tell you straight out. We're losing the place.''

''I can't say I'm surprised.''

''I do the book work. The ranch is slipping away.''

''Still open range around here?''

''Oh it's open range all right.''

He caught her meaning. ''Been losing head?''

''Not much,'' she admitted.

''Rustlers?''

She didn't look at him. ''Yeah,'' she said. ''Rustlers.''

''You don't believe that,'' he said.

''Sure I do. I believe in rustlers who only come around when my cash is low and his bottles are empty.''

''Benjy? But he's stealin' from himself. Don't he see that?''

She shrugged. ''He has expensive tastes. I suppose he doesn't want to wait until we can build up a good-sized herd.'' She laid a cautious hand on his arm. ''You know, Don, I haven't been able to talk to anybody like you for a long time.''

''Anybody like me? How can I help? I don't see how I can help.''

''I guess I don't either,'' she said testily as she stood. ''But it helps just to talk sometimes.'' She started for the window again but changed her mind. ''You mean there's nothing you can think of? You're a stockman, aren't you? You're here on cattle business—or was it gold mining?''

Brax pushed himself away from the table. ''Ma'am,'' he

began carefully, "I thank you for the meal."

"Wait, please, I'm sorry, I didn't mean to get saucy."

"My business here is mine and Vicente's," Brax muttered.

"Yes, yes of course, I accept that. I'm sorry."

Brax took her arm, a little more roughly than he meant to.
"Kat, listen . . ." This woman stirred a lot more in him than
his manhood. And that's what bothered him so much. Didn't
he have enough on his mind? Just out of lockup, a marked
man in a hardcase town. Harv Jordan's town. Brax stared at
Benjy's woman. Her eyes were soft and shiny. Reflected in
their pale blue he fancied he could see the far hills. What did
he owe Benjy anyway? Nothing. No, that wasn't so. He
owed him no less than any other man. And what would he
owe this woman after he let her open up to him? It would be
best, for now, to stick to the business at hand. He let go of her
arm.

"Look, Benjy may not be much of a cowpuncher but
surely the two of you can keep track of a couple of hundred
head. And I'll help with fall roundup. I'd enjoy that. When
do you expect the crew out here?"

"Crew? There'll be no crew."

"No crew? But you'll be needing a little help for the fall
roundup. Can't you get a few cowhands from town?"

"They'd have to work on promise."

"That's the way it's usually done."

"Not around here it isn't."

"But this place . . ." He spread his arms. "It's magnificent."

"It's all changed now. John had good credit."

"The land's not free and clear?"

"Not by a long ways." She stepped over to the woodburner and began to flutter about the kitchen, stacking pots,
arranging spices, anything to keep her hands busy. She
stopped abruptly and faced him. "Don, he won't even tell me
who holds the loan! Some bank over in Cedar is what he says
but when I ask to see the papers he puts me off."

"I don't understand this." She was the most exciting woman he had ever met.

She lowered her eyes. "Benjy was working here when John died. And then it was springtime, things were greening up again. I had to go on living."

"You don't have to. . ."

"I want to. Benjy had good looks. He made me laugh again. He kept the night away." She dared a glance into his eyes. "I know what you must be thinking."

"I'm thinkin' nothing. Way I see it, the harder a man looks at others the less he's willing to look at himself. I'm not about to judge."

She waited for more but he was finished. "Well," she floundered, "it wasn't like that right away. Anyway, after a while he just sort of took over. I mean I let him. That summer was a hot dry one, but the wells flowed just as John planned. Only this time no pasture went in, no garden like before." She threw up her hands. "Oh damn it! If I can just get those papers I can sell off a little, hang on to most of it. This place, it's my home now, it's my *querencia*, the home range. Vicente would understand."

Brax took her hand in his callused brown paw. "I understand. I grew up on a place like this. We didn't have a big fancy house or more than one, but it's the same thing, Katheryn." What would it have been like, those four years, if a woman like this was waiting? Would the rocks have broke a little easier, would the mud-filled carts have weighed a little less? He wanted to blurt it out, make her see what it could have meant. But of course he couldn't do that.

"He pays a bill now and again," she was saying. "I don't even want to guess where the money comes from. But it seems to bother him."

"The Benjy I knew wasn't a bad man," Brax said.

"Neither was the one I used to know. I'd like to think that's still so but I simply can't believe anything he tells me anymore."

Brax caught himself staring at her and he hastily averted

his eyes to the window. "Katheryn, I've got problems of my own. Big problems."

"You're on the run," she stated flatly.

Brax let her hand drop and leaned back so two chairlegs were in the air. "Vicente's right about this place needing repairs. Nothin' a couple of men couldn't handle in a few days though. I notice you don't have much hay up. A hard winter could be trouble. Don't know this country too well but I can see it's high enough for a big snow."

"Sure, Don, but let's not play-act with each other, O.K.? If we have to play-act then I'm not interested."

"Not interested? Not interested in what?"

"Look, you want to make like the dumb cowpoke, go ahead. But I'll wager Benjy will be walking through that door any minute now, and then whatever hasn't gotten said won't be."

"All right. What exactly is it you want from me, anyway?"

"Don, this ranch was John's dream. His whole life. Well he's gone now and I'm not one to live in the past. But if I lose this there'll be nothing." She stood over him, put her arms around his neck. "Maybe you're an outlaw, maybe not. I like your looks and I like your style, but if I have to sweet-talk you to get you to help, I will. And if I have to—"

He made a half-hearted attempt to free himself. "Look, Kat, all I can do is . . . I'll tell you if he says anything about the papers. He's a talker when he drinks."

"You notice that's all the time now."

"More than that I can't promise." He gently pushed her away and stood. "And I don't need no promises from you, understand? I'm just passing through."

She followed him to the door. "I'm going to send him away."

"You think he'll go?"

"No." She stood still before him.

Brax didn't fight it. His long arms circled her and he kissed her. And again, until the sounds of hooves and clanging gear separated them. Her hand slipped from his and Benjy walked into the kitchen.

"Thanks for lunch, Ma'am," Brax said. Unflustered, Katheryn went about her kitchen chores.

"Brax, I need help driving a couple of mavericks," Benjy said.

"That was a quick trip to town. Get what you needed?"

Benjy was already on his way out. "Yeah. Let's go."

They walked to the barn to get Brax's mare. Vicente was scabbing a weak fence rail at the main corral. He did not look up as they passed. "Let's get the kid," Brax suggested. "He might enjoy this."

"Don't take but two of us, Brax. I see he's doin' some patch-up work. Let's leave him be. 'Course, you boys will be paid for your work. No more than other hands, no less."

"A roof and grub is pay enough." Brax climbed into the saddle. "Where are those strays?"

Benjy pointed towards Lodgepole. "See that saddle in the land yonder?" He indicated a forested dip among the foothills. "All-year stream. You know how cattle are. Rather starve to death by water than walk a hundred yards to grass."

"Let's go get 'em, partner."

They passed Vicente once more on the way out and again he did not seem to see them. As soon as their backs were to him he dropped his tools and quick-stepped across the yard to the kitchen door. He entered without knocking and glided past Katheryn who was emptying a bucket into the kitchen basin. Vicente mumbled apologies but did not stop, going through the kitchen and down the hall to the guest room.

He checked the lever-action on his Winchester and stuffed the magazine to its capacity of fifteen cartridges, then adjusted his holster and inspected the cylinder of his revolver, a .44 caliber that could fire the same bullets as the old rifle. He pulled his knife and his whetstone and ran the blade over the stone. Satisfied, he jogged to the barn and saddled up the roan.

*       *       *

"Jordan!" Tores knocked again, more forcefully. "Open up, goddamn it!"

Jordan dragged himself out of the chair and stumbled to the door. "Who is it?" he managed.

"Who the hell do you think it is—Don Braxton?"

"Franklin?"

"Open up!"

Jordan opened the door. He swayed and threw a hand against the jamb to steady himself. "What is it?"

"You wanted to see me before we left. Say, what's wrong with you?"

"Nothing. What time is it?" He fumbled for his pocket watch, found it, and squinted at its face. "You're late. You better get going. How many men?"

"There're four of us."

"Don't take Billy," Jordan said quietly.

"I aim to enjoy my money. I'm not going up against him with less. Tell you what, big man, why don't *you* take his place?"

"I don't feel well."

"You don't feel well or you don't feel brave?"

Jordan gathered himself. "You are wasting precious time."

The door slammed and Harv Jordan was alone again.


They rode over the grassy rolling range into the wooded foothills.

"Benjy, it don't take a wise man to see you're not near ready for winter."

"Is that so?" Benjy brought his mount to a halt. "If it don't suit you here, Brax, why don't you head on back to Yuma?"

"No call to get huffy, partner. You know I been around cattle a long time. I can help you if you don't fight me. What the hell's eating you, anyway? Maybe I can help you keep this damn place."

His look softened. "Sure, Brax. Don't pay me no mind. Been kind of edgy lately. Distracted."

"What about winter feed?"

"That's what the trip to town was. To see about layin' in stores."

"Can you get hay in town?"

"Sure, Brax."

"What about fall roundup?" Brax persisted.

"Fall roundup?" Benjy thought for a moment, then leaned out of the saddle. He tapped Brax on the chest and poked himself over the heart. "This here's it!"

Brax let it ride. Benjy led them to a channel scoured smooth by centuries of flood waters. They followed the trickle downstream. The riverbed dropped but the land didn't, and soon they were winding their way through dry-bottom country hedged in by terraced canyon walls.

"Benjy, we been riding a long time. You sure you got the right canyon?"

"I was out here only last week."

From his saddle Brax studied the moving ground. "No sign. No chewed brush, no droppings, nothing."

"We ain't there yet," Benjy snapped. They rode on in silence until Benjy pointed up a side canyon to where a feeble tributary fed the main watercourse. "This here runs into some pretty rough country but it's worth a look for the first mile or so. I'll go on up the fork. Straight ahead's where I seen 'em last. You run into 'em, give a hoot. I'll do the same."

"Benjy, if my old trail boss is right, it takes a special gift to smell out lost cattle. And partner, I don't think you've got it."

Benjy managed a grin. "Maybe that's so, Brax. If you get to the dropoff and don't see 'em, just wait on me. It's a real pretty little waterfall, you can't miss it." He headed his mount up the side canyon and out of sight.

Brax rode on slowly, dismounting every hundred yards or so to check the sand. Nothing. Oh there were tracks all right—skunk, badger, fox—but no cattle. And the tracks weren't fresh either; cow prints couldn't have been washed away by a flood. Brax was certain now Benjy was wrong. If he had seen the missing cattle it wasn't here. Maybe he'd been drinking and got the location mixed up.

Benjy wasn't the only one who was mixed up. Against his better judgment Brax had come to Lodgepole, knowing full well he was riding into trouble—exactly what he'd vowed not to do as he sat night after night in his tiny cell in Yuma, reviewing his life and trying to figure how to do it better once he got out. That damn Vicente, he was so persuasive. So full of the life Brax feared had been drained out of him. And now on top of it all *she* played on his mind, like a sweet dream snatched away by morning's light.

Brax brought himself back to the business at hand. This did seem like the kind of draw that would attract strays. It was plenty wide—at least forty yards wall to wall. Was that a cow print? He climbed down again for a better look. It was a hoof, all right, but not a steer's. Probably a big pronghorn. Man who spends a decade breathing trail dust and cattle dung knows a cow print when he sees one. He had his hand on the pommel and was lifting himself into the saddle when the rider appeared on the bank ten feet above, a short-barreled, double-tube scattergun rested in the crook of his arm.

The shotgun sprang erect as both hammers were cocked. Brax froze in mid-swing. "That's smart, cowboy," the rider said. "Now let's see both boots on solid ground."

Brax dropped to his feet. From the opposite bank came a voice, calm and sweet. "Don Braxton." A man on foot stepped out of the thickets that shielded a gap in the canyon walls. "You're under arrest for the murder of Ernie Keppman."

That face, chiseled from chalk, could belong only to the man called Tores. A third gunman appeared on horseback near the shotgunner. "Hello, Billy," Brax said to him, and a fourth appeared on the opposite bank.

A grin crossed Billy Ferson's moronic face and he shrugged. Just doin' his job. He held a long-barreled pistol fitted with a shoulder stock and he pointed it at Brax's heart. These boys were taking no chances.

Tores pulled Brax's Colt out of the holster and tossed it into the sand. "So you're Braxton," he said, studying his face. Brax stared back into tiny remorseless eyes. Brax had known such men before, their dull gazes stained with needless death. Tores whistled once and the mounted man on the far bank coaxed his horse down the slope into the wash. He dismounted and patted Brax down in search of a knife or a pocket pistol. Then he reached into the back pocket of his Levis and pulled out a pair of handcuffs.

"You're working for Jordan, aren't you, Tores?" Brax wanted to laugh at this grotesque desperado. "He must be paying you well. Do you know what he is? Do you, Tores? Maybe you're the same way."

"Don't bait me, Braxton. It might work with Billy but not me." He took the handcuffs from his companion. "You do have a choice here, you know. You can come peaceful or you can come dead."

It was high time. The odds would be worse if he waited until Brax was shackled. Vicente inched his way down from the upper terraces to the ledge directly above and behind the man with the shotgun. The thick mantel of tamarisk had shielded him but now he was in the open. All eyes were on Brax but should one man's view wander to the banks Vicente would be dead in the time it took to pull a trigger.

He straightened out of his crouch, brought the butt of his rifle down with a blow meant to kill. There was a sharp crack as the skull broke, and the force knocked the Winchester from Vicente's hands. The man teetered, for a moment his shotgun seemed to prop him up against the saddle, then he slowly pitched forward. Vicente dropped onto the horse and wrested the scattergun from limp hands before the man slid over the horse's neck to land face-first in the riverbed.

Billy saw it coming. Vicente jerked the shotgun to his shoulder and let go with both barrels. The upper part of Billy Ferson gaped crimson, the horse reared, Billy's feet caught in the stirrups. The panicked mount bolted for the woods, a bloody ragdoll flopping in the saddle. Tores went for his gun. Brax whirled on his heels and struck out as hard as he could. The blow cracked Tores's jaw and sent him into the other gunman. Brax scrambled to the safety of the boulders but not before the men got to their feet and threw shots that whined off the face of the rocks and kicked grit into his face.

Vicente dropped the scattergun and tossed his revolver. Brax one-handed it, firing as he turned. The barrage sent Tores and his partner scurrying. They made it to the opposite bank and returned the fire as Vicente groped the ledge above him. He found the Winchester and pumped the lever with dizzying speed, raining deadly fire across the gulley, pinning down Tores and his man. That put an end to their wild shooting and silence closed in.

Brax reloaded the .44 while Vicente crouched behind scanty cover and waited for a target. Tores and the gunman huddled and dared not show themselves. Tores could possibly work his way back, through the cleft and out of the canyon where his horse waited. His partner risked a peek over the boulders, saw nothing. Tores pointed. There, to the left—was that movement in the brush? The halfbreed was working his way over, trying to surround them. The gunman leaned far out to get a clear shot. He took careful aim. Brax was ready for him. Before he could squeeze the trigger Brax sent a .44 screaming through his brain.

"Ready to give up, Sheriff?"

But Tores wasn't listening. He was getting the hell out. Backing up, half-crawling, anything to put ground between himself and them. It was only twenty yards to the thickets. He made a run for it.

Tores was a man running the gauntlet; he was quick on the sprint, crouching low and dodging from side to side. Vicente

rose from the bushes, Winchester at his shoulder, and
squeezed off a shot. He was so sure that he lowered the rifle to
watch the man die.

For the second time since Brax had known him Vicente's
aim failed.

Tores vanished in the brush. By the time they realized what
was happening the sound of hoofbeats was being swallowed
by the forest.

"Come on, Brax!"

Brax shook his head and pointed to a spreading spot of
blood on his left forearm. It was not serious, a graze from a
ricocheted bullet. Vicente swore as he washed the wound
with stream water and rigged up a bandage. Brax was quiet.
He shook his head in wonder.

"Of course I followed you," Vicente said peevishly. "Do
you think I would let you ride into the forest alone? With
*him?*"

"Did you actually see Benjy with them?"

He answered as though scolding a child. "Señor Brax, if I
had followed him instead of you, we would not now be
having this chat, eh?" He took in the canyon with a sweep of
his arm. "Excellent ambush country, no?"

"Kid, I take it all back, about the book learning, and—"

"This is no book learning, this is my uncle's teaching.
Each time I ran away from the Brothers, and that was often,
he took me, and taught me the ways of war."

Brax pointed to the man who had been rifle-butted. "What
about him?" He nudged the still form with the toe of his boot,
then turned him over. "This guy's dead." Brax found the
hole in the temple where a bullet had entered. "You shoot
him? I didn't shoot him."

"Stray bullet?"

"They shot one of their own men."

Brax followed Vicente to the meadow where the roan had
grazed peacefully through the battle. "You are all right
then?" Vicente asked. "I don't come back to the ranch. I will

meet you at last night's camp.''

Brax couldn't believe his ears. ''You're going after him? Ain't you had enough?''

''Tores, he will run to Lodgepole. I cannot hope to catch him in the open. I don't know this land. But it is time one of us had a looksee at this Lodgepole, no?''

''We'll both go. I'm not hurt.''

''Ah, but you forget.''

''Benjy.''

Vicente pulled himself into the saddle. ''Your escape will be no secret. Señor Benjy he is . . . unstable, I think. And he may be with the Señora.'' He stopped him with a wave of his hand. ''You need say nothing. I know how you feel about her. And you know as well what I think fitting for the Judas. But I do not interfere. I only want the hatchet-face.''

''It's crazy, kid, there may be fifty armed men in town!''

''You think I ride in blowing the bugle? My uncle was Apache. Are we not the world's best sneak thieves?'' He undid the string of his sombrero. ''Give me the Stetson. My hat, it marks me, no?''

''Not much of a disguise, kid.'' He tossed him the hat.

''No, but one needs the light to know me now.''

''God be with you, kid.''

''He has not left us yet.''

''Man makes point only so often. Then he's gotta crap out.''

''Bah! A scouting trip, nothing more! You think *los bobos* can catch *el zorro*? *You* be the careful one, my friend. The villains, they may be at the ranch, or Señor Benjy, he may try to finish this thing, eh? Expect me after moonrise. Adios!'' He roweled the flanks of the roan and took off at a dead run towards Lodgepole.

''Vaya con Dios, kid.''

Dusk had spilled into the valley and out again when Brax topped the rise overlooking the house. From a hundred yards off he saw Katheryn in the window of the brightly-lit kitchen. Benjy's pinto stood loose at the porch rail. Brax left his mare

in a grove of pines and approached on foot. He scouted the
back first and found nothing amiss. Gun drawn, he entered
the kitchen without knocking.

Her hair was undone, a tangled golden mane that reached
to her waist, her face puffy and tear-stained. She saw him and
her eyes widened and her mouth opened but no sound came
out. Instead she ran to him. He gently pried her off. Only her
red-rimmed eyes followed him into the big dark sitting room.

It was a minute or more before his eyes adjusted to the dim
starlight. Benjy sat in the seat he loved so much, staring out
the big south window. He had stayed in the woods, climbed a
hill overlooking the stream. He had seen, and he was waiting.
A bottle lay dead at his feet. Another, a quarter drained,
awaited its fate on the table. He wore his hat but was unarmed. Brax walked in, stopped, and stood over him. He
cocked the Colt and the click of the hammer echoed through
the room. Brax stuck the muzzle of the revolver in his old
partner's ear.

Benjy's eyes, unfocused and unreadable, were glued to the
blur of the window. Brax felt his finger tighten on the trigger,
imagined he could see the cylinder begin its deadly movement. The moment seemed frozen in fresh starlight.

As he watched the broken man before him he was aware
only of the sucking sound the metal made on leather when he
holstered the gun. Benjy turned partway, offering the bottle.
Brax took it, turned it over in his hands. He couldn't read the
label but he knew. Tennessee whisky.

Brax placed the bottle on the table and turned his back.

"Brax," the figure in the darkness croaked. "The title is
in Jordan's safe."

Brax stepped into the glare of the kitchen. "I'll be goin',"
he said to the woman.

"*We*'ll be goin'," Kat said.

"What about him?"

"Later. I've got to get away from here."

She packed nothing. She climbed onto that big black and
white paint and they rode.

# Ten

Harv Jordan always tried to allow a reasonable amount of time for a job, but this wasn't the first time he'd put aside his paperwork and gone to the window. Again he looked at his pocket watch. Only a half an hour had passed since he last caught himself pacing the office and his nerves were being stretched. Already long shadows brought evening to the dusty swath that divided the false fronts of the clapboard buildings. Jordan didn't give much thought to the lone rider from the south who reined in at the Emporium. Most who rode into Lodgepole stopped here.

Breathless, Tores looped the reins over the front rail directly beneath Jordan's window. Jordan squinted, then stared down at the top of his head. Stiff dirty hair ringed a monkish tonsure. Jordan had never seen his hired man hatless. When he reached the landing Tores was already at the bar, hiding his face behind a whisky glass.

"Again!" Tores roared, bringing the glass down on the bar so hard Jordan was sure it had cracked. Tores was uglier than ever. His mouth was swollen and he looked like he'd been on the trail a month. But rage clouded the giant man's judgment. "Tores!" Jordan screamed, and he didn't see Tores move. He did see the drink fly out of his hand and then Tores was in a half-crouch and his hand was filled by a Colt .45. Jordan knew Tores had filed off the guard and rigged a hair trigger. If that pistol went off the lead would pass through Jordan's forehead. Ten yards away was a finger-thick muzzle, a steel-eyed tunnel that could suck Jordan from this world as surely and swiftly as it had so many other men. Jordan wrested his gaze from the deadly hole to the man behind it.

Already some of the fury was draining from that paste-white face. Tores's eyes seemed to focus again. He slipped the revolver back into the holster and swept the bottle off the counter. There were times when whisky lent more courage than guns.

Shaken, Jordan walked back to his office and sat at his desk, leaving the door open behind him. Tores stormed in and slammed it.

"Close, Jordan. Close."

"Take it easy, Franklin," he said gently. "Sit down a minute, cool off."

"Goddamn it!" Tores slammed his fist into the chair.

"You've handled many jobs for me, Franklin," Jordan began carefully. "What is it that makes this one so different?"

"He's got an Apache or somethin'." Tores shook his head. "I never seen anything like it." He took a long swallow of whisky. "Shit! Three of the best guns in the county dead."

"Dead?" Was Jordan surprised, really? He'd seen only the failure of the mission, not the whole picture. First Braxton guns down Ernie, now Billy. "Damn!" A stab of remorse cut through him, and he wondered if he was more disgusted with the turn of events or the pity he felt. How could he mourn Billy Ferson, that moron? Because Billy

looked up to him? Like a little boy and his pa. Jordan thought
of the black brick in his safe. No. It had taken him all day to
pull himself together.

"Five thousand for Braxton, dead or alive." He sprang to
his feet. "It goes to any man that brings him down. I'm sorry,
that means you'll have competition now. And I want you to
take care of that Thomas character. Maybe he tipped off the
Indian."

"Jordan, you ever think maybe this thing is getting out of
hand?"

"And I'll pay another thousand to the man that brings in
that Indian."

"What the hell," said Tores, and he took another soothing
pull off the bottle. The pain of the jaw was subsiding at last.

"That goddamn Thomas." Jordan was pacing rapidly.
"He seemed on the level. Why didn't he say anything about a
bodyguard?"

"He's a drunk. Maybe forgot." Tores put down the bottle.
Any more and he wouldn't be able to work. "Let me ask you
something. What in holy hell this Braxton ever do to you?"

Jordan whirled. "What did Braxton do to me? I'll show
you what, goddam you!" He ripped off the eyepatch and the
gaping socket leered at the astonished gunman. The hole had
never closed. It had simply lined itself with crusty death-gray
scar tissue.

Even Tores recoiled. No one had seen Jordan without the
patch and now he knew why.

Shamed, Jordan turned away. He regretted the dramatic
gesture. He had stood naked before this contemptible killer.
He replaced the patch and sit down.

Frank Tores spoke with some gentleness. "Look here, Mr.
Jordan, I got a score to settle too. Braxton's the toughest one I
ever had. Next time I got to be ready for anything." He
paused to let it sink in. "I need more men, understand? I've
got to have firepower. This thing calls for. . ."

"Extraordinary measures."

"Like I just told you, this thing's become personal to me."

"Sure it's personal. Five thousand dollars' worth of personal." He smacked his fist against his palm. "The man that kills him gets the money. Or the one that's left to tell the tale, have it any way you want. Now get the hell out of here and don't come back without that bastard's head."

Tores leaped to his feet. "I don't see *you* ridin' out against those killers. No, you just sit back and spread the money. You're yellow, Jordan."

Jordan hurled his bulk out of the chair and at him. Again Tores's Colt seemed to appear out of the air. Jordan stopped, sank back into the big chair. "Franklin, the next time you point that thing at me you better intend to use it."

Tores headed for the door.

"So you think I'm yellow, eh?" Jordan shouted at his back. "You bring me Braxton, I'll kill him personally. That's how I *want* it. Bring him alive and I'll make you rich. Ten thousand. You can have the Harris ranch. Take the woman. You'd like that best of all, wouldn't you?"

Tores did not face him. "You'll have him," he said calmly. "Alive. And I'll see you keep those promises. And then they'll be one further piece of business. Between you and me, savvy?" He snorted and slammed the door shut behind him.


He'd been turning the options over and decided. It was best to kill this Jordan, and the sooner the better. Just a name to him, but Vicente was betting his life it was he who sent the assassins. And Brax knew why. Something bound those two together, something horrible out of the hellhole of Yuma. And now that Vicente rode with Brax and killed at his side, he too was linked by that awful chain. He'd have to ask Jordan about it before he shot him.

And Brax? What did he have in mind? He seemed to have no plan, was unwilling to face this thing head on to or take steps to protect himself. What was he thinking of now aside from Katheryn.

Would Katheryn keep Brax from killing the traitor? Or some foolish regard for the past? The hell with that. Benjy should be given to the Apaches.

If tonight went well this would be the end of it. If not, would Brax carry it through, or would he run? A woman could push a man either way. Still Vicente had a feeling she was all right. Benjy was one of her few mistakes. Brax and Katheryn would not make a team of cowards.

"I'm sorry," she said. They were setting up camp in the copse where they had first met.

"It was something he just couldn't turn down."

"But he betrayed you. An old friend."

"Yes."

"Most men would have killed him."

Brax searched for kindling. "I'm not the hangman," he said, stepping into the darkness of the brush. "I don't kill unarmed men."

"Could he have sensed?"

There was the rustle of branches and the sound of snapping twigs and he reappeared with an armload of wood. "Sensed what, Katheryn?"

"You know . . . us." A tiny spluttering flame licked the sticks. Brax blew into the fire and it swelled, flooding the tiny clearing. The dancing firelight played on her face. She lowered her head and glanced into the shadows. "He saw the fight. He said, 'It's all over. Brax and the kid beat them.' It's you and me now, Don, isn't it?"

A raven squawked. Brax followed its soaring flight, over a break in the pines and out of sight. The raven. To the Indian a wily trickster, a creature to be admired. To the white man, a symbol of death. For the first time he thought of the three bodies in the north canyon.

"Damn it, it's enough to make my head spin." She turned from him and spoke to the night. "He *was* good to me, once." She whirled and kicked at the dirt. "The damn thing is I can't even tell how I feel. Relieved, now that it's come to a head? Or what? I don't know. Awful, I guess. That's how I feel. No, that's not right, I look at you and I feel happy. And scared, too. I don't even know you. And I don't even know how you feel about me."

Brax looked away from the flames to her face. The fire shined on her tears. "Yes you do," he said.

She knelt beside him, and touched his cheek. "I don't know what this is all about. But I know it's not over." She rose and her tone lightened. "Can I help with the camp?" Brax shook his head and stoked the fire. "Do you think we're safe?" She was talking now to keep the quiet from pressing in on them. "Do you think it's safe here? This is where Benjy got the drop on Vicente."

"The kid was thinkin' again," Brax grunted. "Gets in his way sometimes."

Once more she knelt beside him. "The Indians say they can smell a man's fear in his sweat. Think that's so?"

"I don't know. Ask the kid. If we ever see him again."

"I think maybe a woman—I think a woman can read a man's fight in his eyes."

He looked straight at her. "Not this fight, Katheryn."

Neither moved during the silence that followed. "And I think," Brax said as he reached for her. "I think you are the most beautiful woman I've ever known." He cupped her face in his hands. With great feeling he kissed her damp lips. Gently she broke his embrace and moved back just far enough to look upon his whole face. "You knew I wanted to do that again, didn't you?" he said.

"I did." She sat upright and tugged at the drawstrings of her blouse. The garment parted smoothly and the firelight bronzed her tawny breasts. Brax caressed them gingerly, as if fearful they would shatter. Her nipples stiffened beneath his fingers. Absurdly, the image of a rain-swelled cactus flashed into his mind.

"I could love you. I know I could. Maybe I already do."

"You don't have to say that, Don." She stood and, as Brax looked on, undid her denim skirt and let it slide down over her sleek hips to the ground. She wore underpants of fine silk, the color of her eyes and a Utah sky. Brax sprang to his feet. He placed his hands on her hips and tugged on her undergarment. Before she could step out of them he put both hands between her legs. He curled the little hairs around his fingers and stroked and probed her.

With a quick, practiced motion she undid his belt buckle as he tossed off his course linen range shirt. She helped him out of his breeches then stepped back again, this time to look him up and down. She liked what she saw and smiled. A night breeze passed through the camp, stirring the pine needles that littered the ground, making them shiver.

She pushed him down onto his back and then lowered herself on top of him. Her face, flushed and shiny in the light of the dancing fire, glowed a rosy copper.

If someone asked him, Would you keep this moment at the price of all those to come?—he just might have said yes.


Vicente Alvarez tethered the roan safely in a dark alley and edged along the decaying walls, his eyes searching for either the hatchet-face he knew or the scarred one he'd heard of. Now and then a solitary horseman drifted up the street and stopped at the only well-lit place in town, Harv's Emporium.

Vicente flitted among the shadows and gained the alley to the rear of the saloon. He climbed the rickety stairs and stood before the back door to Jordan's suite. The door was securely locked. There was no landing along the rear window and no light seeped through the thick curtains. Maybe he could get in from the front balcony, but he'd have to climb the building wall and he'd be a sitting duck.

*       *       *

Jordan sat in the huge chair behind his desk. A tiny candle flickered, puddling the mahogany desk top with its wax, but he didn't notice. His chin rested on his chest and his eyes were closed. Thick, sour-sweet smoke hung in the air. The jade and ivory pipe his friend Chang had given him lay cool and dirty now by the dying candle.


Vicente strained his ears. Still no sound came from within. Maybe the upper floor was boarded up. He decided not to risk a break-in. He might be courting a fall or a bullet. He slithered around to the front and looked up and down the street. Empty. He pulled Brax's Stetson low and chanced a peak over the batwings through the eye-burning haze of the saloon.

The crowd was a blessing, it meant he would be less conspicuous. There were no familiar faces here and he decided to risk it. There was much to be learned from saloon talk. First he must be sure his mount was handy. When trouble came a man on foot was like a man unarmed. He led the roan from the alley and draped the reins over one of the rails that fronted the Emporium.

Eyes and ears wide open, Vicente entered Jordan's saloon and walked through to the counter where the burly redhead with the thick brogue filled his order for tequila. He drank slowly, took small swallows. He had honed his senses and dared not dull the fine edge.

Red McKormick walked through the doorway of the partition behind his bar into the tiny kitchen. The cook, Tom Gilley, stood idly over his cookstove and basin awaiting food orders. "Take over for me, Tom," the barkeep said. Gilley followed him out of the kitchen, out from behind the bar to the stairs. McKormick turned to him. "See the stranger?" he whispered.

"The greaser, Red?"

"Aye. Don't let him leave. Give him a bottle on the house, shoot him in the leg if you have to, but keep him here."

Vicente watched McKormick as he clomped up the steps and out of sight down the hall. The bartender knocked on the office door and waited, then knocked again, more vigorously. "Mr. Jordan!" he croaked. "Mr. Jordan!" He pounded on the door.

Downstairs Tom Gilley looked past Vicente and saw the batwings part. A man Gilley knew well walked into the saloon and the cook signaled to the new arrival. Vicente, his eyes on the upstairs hallway, backed away from the bar.

"Drink on the house, friend?" Gilley grasped Vicente's arm and splashed his glass to overflowing with tequila. "This here's a wide open town." He placed the bottle in front of him and made to put his free arm around his shoulder. "Men of all colors are welcome." With a mighty shove Vicente sent him crashing into the wall cabinet behind the bar. In two long strides the Mexican was at the foot of the stairs. From there he could see an upstairs door thrown open. McKormick slid inside and the door slammed shut behind him. Vicente's pistol was out and cocked before he climbed the first step. He took the steps two at a time until Frank Tores bounded across the room and laid his head open with the butt of his .45.

Jordan came to the head of the stairs. "Gilley," he called. "Brew me a pot of strong coffee."

Tores addressed some idlers around a table. "Give me a hand with him, boys."

"Never mind," said Jordan thickly, and made his way down the steps. "I can handle him." He hoisted Vicente over his massive shoulders like a sack of flour and headed for the office. Tores followed.

"I spotted the lad first, Mr. Jordan," whined McKormick, appearing at the upper landing. "I knew you was on the lookout for a halfbreed stranger. I spotted the lad first, ask Gilley—"

"Never mind that now, Red. Get back to work."

Jordan shambled up the stairs with his burden. "Tores, the least you can do is get the goddamn door for me." He carried Vicente in and dropped him onto one of the plush office chairs.

"Well, we got this one," said Tores.

"I'll call for you. Close the door behind you."

"What the hell's this, Jordan? I got him for you."

"I'd say there's a couple of Micks downstairs who'd disagree."

Tores dismissed them with a wave of his hand. "Let 'em have the thousand. This bird will lead us to Braxton."

"Franklin, go downstairs, have a drink on the house. We're close now, don't spoil it. Let me speak to him alone." Jordan looked at Vicente's face. "You didn't kill him, did you?"

"Be just your luck if he dies on you!" said Tores, then he stomped out of the room.

Jordan found Vicente's knife. He bathed Vicente's face with a wet towel, tilted his head back and forced a little brandy between his lips. The eyes fluttered and opened. So this was the enemy. Harv Jordan, a one-eyed monster.

"I'm sorry I had to hurt you," the giant said.

"Señor," Vicente managed between shallow breaths. "I am a traveler, far from home. In my land such a man is treated as a guest. He is not hit over the head and carried about."

"If you tell me where he is you can ride out of here. You won't stand trial for the murder of Billy Ferson."

"Murder?"

Now Jordan was pacing. "Tell us how we can get to him and you're free to go," he repeated, reluctant to believe it wasn't going to be this easy.

Vicente's head throbbed viciously. This was to be expected. His vision was clearing and his reflexes returning. He was not badly hurt and could fight. But this Jordan outweighed him by a hundred pounds. And he moved well for such a large man. Vicente scrutinized that face. The hair, beard, and patch left little to study, but the lone eye drew his gaze as an anvil draws a magnet. The eye looked like it was painted on. Vicente had seen such a look in the eyes of Yaqui medicine men during their herb ceremonies. Was this man drugged, or crazy?

"Please." The huge hand reached out and stroked his cheek. Vicente shuddered. "Tell me. I don't want to hurt you anymore." Was the beast actually pleading with him?

"Who is it you search for?" Vicente asked breezily. "I hardly know where I am. How can I tell the whereabouts of another, another whose name you do not even tell me? Señor, you have the wrong man here." He started to rise. "But mistakes happen and I am a forgiving one."

"Sit down!" Jordan shoved him back into the chair so roughly he nearly bounced back up. Fury showed on the sallow face and the veins in the big man's forehead bulged. Jordan planted himself behind the desk. Vicente reached for his knife and cursed, of course it had been taken away. His eyes roamed the room for his blade, a weapon—scissors, anything—but saw none.

"Franklin Tores," Jordan said, "is not a nice man. Must I turn you over to him?"

Of course. The type that pays others to torture and shuts himself away from the screams. Vicente did not blink. With trembling hands Jordan yanked open his desk drawer and pulled out the gun.

"Get up!" Jordan fumbled in the drawer and came up with a ring of keys, pocketed them and seized the kerosene lamp that replaced the used-up candle. "Hands on your head. March straight ahead with small steps. This revolver is a double-action. It's got lead in all six chambers. Turn around once and I'll blow you to pieces."

They walked downstairs. "Sheriff Tores." Jordan was calm now, and spoke for all to hear. "Take this man to jail." Tores pushed the bar away and sauntered over to them. "He won't talk, Franklin," Jordan muttered.

Tores sneered. "Did you think he would?"

"What do you suggest?"

"What I suggest you ain't got the stomach for."

"You have the men?"

"On their way."

The Lodgepole jail was a squat one-room structure of large stones mortared with adobe. The door hung on one rusty hinge and the panes were gone from the windows. Inside a floor-to-ceiling grid of one-inch iron bars ran the width of the building, dividing it evenly into a lawman's office and an eight-by-twelve cell. Jordan found the proper key and turned the lock to the cell. With a painful screak the grid door swung open and Tores thrust in the prisoner. The grate clanged shut and Jordan effortlessly slid a heavy rolltop desk over to the outside entranceway, where it barricaded the broken door.

"Where are those men, Franklin?"

"They'll be here soon. Let's get started."

"No."

Tores looked him up and down. "What's the matter, Harv? 'Fraid you'll puke on your fancy suit?"

"I don't want you touching him, Tores, hear me?" Jordan's voice cracked. "We'll leave him here awhile, let him stew alone."

They took the lantern with them. Vicente waited for his eyes to adjust to the faint light admitted by the windows. He should have gone to the ranch first, and forced the traitor Benjy to tell all. Brax was right to be cautious.

Because a man did not fill his straight, was he therefore a fool for drawing? Vicente examined his prison. Any other town would have lights in its police station and in its streets. But this was no town, it was a ghost encampment. It was Jordan's circus or would be. Only Katheryn's ranch was decent and clean, once the Judas was gone. And that, thanks to Vicente's impetuousness, might never be. There was no time for such thoughts. He scoured every inch of the cell. Iron bars held up well in this climate. The weakest part of the structure was the crumbling mortar between the stones. Hopeless. Even if he could chip away all the mud the smallest of the stones would take the strength of Jordan to budge. He removed a spur and scratched at the earth. Rock hard. It could take days to dig out. Vicente started digging.

The street door opened and a lantern hung there in the night. Then the men filed in—Jordan, Tores, and four others. Without a word Jordan turned the lock of the cell and two men stepped in. Vicente hid the spur behind his back. There was no doubt what was to occur.

With the speed of a coiled diamondback he struck. The spur ripped one man's cheek open to the bone. He howled and dropped to the dirt. Vicente spun and drove the spur into the other man's temple, then charged head-first into the crowd, smashing into Tores's gut and knocking the wind out of him. He bowled another one down before he lost his footing. Then he scrambled to his feet and collided into Jordan, who might have been the stone walls of his prison.

Vicente flailed and kicked but it was useless, they were all over him. He was hauled to his feet and they slammed him back against the cell bars. They forced his arms back and handcuffed them together.

He sat on the floor of the office, his back up against the iron grate, hands manacled behind him through the bars.

"Get his feet!" Someone produced a rope and tied his legs.

"So now you torture me, eh, you cowards? All these big men to keep one little Mexican, eh, you filthy scum?" The kerosene-fed flame flickered wildly in the drafty room, making moving paintings of their staring faces. "I will live to piss on your graves, you bastardos!"

"Tores, come here," said Jordan, and the two men walked outside. Jordan leaned against the broken door. "Take one good man and go to the ranch."

"You really think Braxton's fool enough to go there?"

Jordan shrugged. "We haven't second-guessed the son of

a bitch yet. Who knows what he'll do? Maybe he'll go take
care of Thomas.''

"And if he doesn't?''

"We can't have Thomas around. We agreed on that.''

"*We* didn't agree on nothin'. That's extra. No fancy deals.
Plus the thousand for the Mex.''

"The bartender fingered him. I owe him that.''

"Let's kill him, too.''

"I don't think you're funny, Tores.''

"Well I want to be here when the greaseball sells out
Braxton. I want to hear him squeal like a stuck pig.''

Sure you do. The spunky kid bested you and you can't
stand that. You'd love to see him suffer. That's reason
enough to get you out of here. You might kill him before he
talked. "Long as you work for me, Tores, you take orders.
Look, who's the best man to cover the ranch?'' He jerked his
head towards the door. "Those clowns in there would be
blown out of the saddle as soon as they topped the rise.
Remember, bring me Braxton alive and the price is doubled.''

Tores bared his yellow teeth. "All right. Business before
pleasure, I suppose.''

You could still use the bastard's greed against him. Mention money and he's agreeable.

Tores opened the door and stepped back inside. The men
were passing around a bottle and awaiting instructions.
"Juan Mondregas, you come with me. Rest of you boys take
your orders from Mr. Jordan here. Lester. . .''

From out of the shadows a death's head emerged. Vicente
stared at Lester's face, gaunt and hollow with thin bloodless
lips and deep eye sockets. "You boys let up when he talks,''
said Jordan. "Any man who doesn't won't be paid.'' Lester
nodded. The flame of the lantern glinted off the steel of his
Bowie knife. "No cutting yet,'' Jordan said. Lester sheathed
the blade, stepped back, and kicked Vicente in the groin.

Jordan squelched the urge to walk in circles. Why doesn't

he talk? Why doesn't the kid stop them? Tores is right. I don't
have the stomach for this.

"The face last," Jordan said, and walked out into the
autumn night.

# Eleven

Stars blazed in the inky sky. The pinyon fire danced itself into fragrant embers while the bedroll kept the night's chill at bay. A rustle of wings followed an owl's hoot and something—perhaps an unwary pack rat—felt the stab of talons. The rat sank into extinction and somewhere in the slickrock coyotes gossiped. Brax awoke with a start. To sleep was to invite danger. A sliver of a moon was up. Brax searched the sky and noted the position of the Dipper. It was a habit acquired from long watch on the cattle trails. Vicente had left at sundown.

"Katheryn." Gently he shook her.

She shushed him with a finger on his lips. "You owe me nothing, understand?"

"I'm going to look for the kid."

"What?" She shook off the sleep that made her voice husky. "You're leaving?"

"Got to. I can't believe he'd be this late."

"Those people—Jordan, that awful man Frank—it's them, isn't it? I know of them. There's been lots of talk. They're outlaws. They're bastards."

"I know that."

"Anything involving them can't be good."

"This ain't."

She sat up and the bedroll slipped to her waist. "I should pray to God you're not here for banditry or murder."

"I'll do no innocent man harm."

She placed her hands on his shoulders. "No innocent man? Who decides?"

Brax cupped her breasts. "You are so pretty. You're beautiful. You are."

She lifted his hands and pushed them away. "I mean it, Don. Who decides who's innocent? You?"

Brax tossed aside the bedroll and stood. "I'll be going then." He picked up his trousers and stepped into them.

"You have a most infuriating way of not hearing questions you don't like!"

"All right then. *I* decide. Since the Law won't." Brax checked the chambers of his revolver and tested the hammer action.

"But have you tried?" She was on her feet. "Look, I know about the ambush in the wash. Benjy didn't have to say anything, I could hear it. They'd have killed you if they could. Have you thought of telling an honest lawman? Would you settle for justice?"

"Justice?" He sighed. "The law and justice have little in common."

"Do you really believe that?"

"I do." He slid on his boots and buttoned the last button of his shirt. "And as for looking for justice," he said as he untied the mare, "that's hardly first on the list here. 'Less you can see a certain justice in keeping me alive." He stepped into the stirrup and pulled himself up, sat for a moment high in the saddle looking down at her. "Kat . . ." he began, then faltered. The thought of leaving her alone here was painful.

She read his fears. "I can take care of myself." She walked over to the big black and white paint and pulled the

rifle from the saddle boot. "Benjy's. It's a Winchester '76."
She stood, naked in the thin mountain night, and held the
weapon out to him.

"You better hold on to that. I never was much with a long
gun anyway. Can you shoot?"

She quieted his fears at once. She pumped the lever arm of
the repeater and raised the gun to firing position with the fluid
motion of experience.

Brax was ready to ride. "I'd sooner stay and go another
round with you, lady."

"I'm sure. What the hell *are* you going to do?"

"Maybe nothing, but I'll do all I can. I'll start by looking
for him."

"Brax, come here. Lean over." He did. "More, you
dumb Texas dust-eater!" She pulled his face down, close to
hers, folded her gentle hands over his ears and kissed him.

"May God watch over you, cowboy."

"Hup!" And the gray mare, who worked for him as
though she'd never known another rider, carried him out of
the clearing, over the rise, and out of sight.

The trail to Lodgepole was a good one, almost a road, and
even in the dark Brax could handle it at a canter. On the
mountainside he sighted the faint glow of the town and his
thoughts raced ahead of the flying hooves. If he's dead,
Tores, Jordan, anyone mixed up in this will taste my lead.
The determination clicked something inside, brought a feeling of righteousness. Until the old doubts came back, the
need to step back and look at everything so damn logically,
study all the angles. No, I can't get away from it. If Vicente is
dead it's my fault. Not just because this was Brax's fight but
because he had hedged, put off decisions, done nothing. The
kid wouldn't wait, couldn't. And Vicente was right. It's the
dozing bird that gets blown out of the nest. Five years back
Brax would have taken care of this thing quick and proper.
Found out who was after him and blasted the bastards into the
nearest boot hill.

But that was before Yuma.

Only a few lights illuminated Lodgepole and its ram-
shackle buildings. Here and there, in front of the supply store
and the livery, lanterns hung from poles. Brax recalled what
tempting targets they made for pistol-toting cowpunchers
celebrating the end of a long drive. The saloon, of course,
glowed warm and cheery and an occasional barroom sound
drifted his way but the town was quiet. Harv's never burst its
seams anymore, not like it did during the short-lived gold
rush.

Brax tethered the mare behind the livery and made his way
towards the saloon. He stopped and scanned the length of the
storefront boardwalk. The only men he saw were lying on the
plank walkway in that fronted the Emporium, or in the dust of
the street, dead drunk in the cold.

He edged his way around the back, climbed the same stairs
Vicente had taken, came to the same locked rear door and the
same conclusion. He paced the gloomy alleyways, shivering.
The dark side streets made him feel low, a creature hiding
from the light. There was only one thing left to do. He pulled
Vicente's sombrero low and turned up his coat collar. Holding his breath, and his gun, he dared a look over the swinging
doors into the Emporium. Rapidly his eyes played over each
patron. None were known to him. He faced the street again.
To walk in there would be suicide. This was Jordan's town
and Jordan's saloon. And *that* was Vicente's horse!

I will assume he's alive until I learn different. He
examined the horse. There were many roans but few saddles
like this one. Indecision gnawed as he flattened himself
against the wall. There was no other way. He'd have to enter
Harv's and demand information at gunpoint. He checked the
Colt and studied the street once more.

Across the way and two hundred yards to the south faint
light seeped from the street windows of the old jail. That's
what it would take to hold a wildcat like Vicente, iron bars
and stone walls. The jail was closed, Brax had heard, because
officially the town was abandoned. Then why was a light

burning? Had "Sheriff" Tores moved in? Brax slunk over to the dilapidated structure. Voices, low and muffled, came from within. There was more in this stone box than a light.

Warily he tested the door. It gave an inch before jamming against the rolltop. He heard a thud, more voices. Was that a moan? The sound of splashing water? The windows were high and recessed. Brax pulled himself onto the ledge and peered inside.

Water dripped from Vicente. A man was putting down a bucket. Another squatted beside him, drinking from a bottle. And the third loomed over Vicente with a knife. Shirtless, Vicente sat in a puddle of blood. A stripe two inches wide ran from his shoulder to his stomach. A raw furrow where skin had been sliced off.

Brax flung the door outwards, the hinge tore from the jamb and he fired even as they turned. The first one got his hand as far as the butt of the pistol in his belt when his chest was blown apart; he was dead before he hit the floor. Lester whirled and the knife flew from his fingers. The blade thunked into the rosewood desk and sank nearly to the hilt. Brax needed no more surprises. He thumbed back the hammer, pointed the gun at Lester's head, and squeezed the trigger. The bullet shattered his bony face and sent him sprawling against the bars.

The last one sprang to his feet, his head swinging wildly about as if in search of a way out. Brax saw the crude bandage on his cheek and the look of wild fear in his eyes. Reason flashed dimly through his fury, and he opened his mouth to shout at the bastard, make him throw those hands in the air. But the man, thinking there could be no mercy, went for his gun, and Brax drilled him between the eyes.

Brax hurtled the desk and knelt by his friend. Vicente smiled broadly and nodded his head in appreciation of a job well done. "The keys," he gasped, "Jordan has them."

"By God, they'll pay for this!" Brax leaned over into the cell and put the muzzle of his still-smoking pistol against the short length of chain that bound his friend's hands. "Pull tight, kid." He fired and the links disintegrated. Brax pulled the knife from the desk. Vicente snatched it from his hands and sliced the rope that held his feet.

"Stay put!" Brax shouted. "You want to bleed to death?"

Vicente ignored him, scooped up the bottle and gulped greedily as he crawled over the bodies. He took a revolver and the deerskin sheath that held the knife while Brax tore his own shirt into bandages. Brax grabbed the bottle and wet the cloth with high-proof liquor. "Hang on, kid." He daubed the wound and the fire of the spirits almost made Vicente faint. "Gotta be done," Brax muttered. "Hurt much?"

"Does more good inside," Vicente replied, and downed three more ounces as Brax hastily bandaged him. He grimaced at the taste. "When will you gringos learn to drink?"

"Enough liquor!" Brax seized the bottle and smashed it against the wall. "Can you ride?"

"We kill Jordan, yes?"

"You're delirious." Brax wrapped his arm around him and pulled him to his feet. They hobbled outside and down the alley to the back of the livery.

"My horse, Brax!"

"You can't ride alone." They heard shouts and running feet. The carnage had been discovered.

"We are an army, no? A soldier must have his steed!"

"Can't risk it! We'll get another." Brax was up on the mare. "Climb on, we got to get the holy hell out of here!"

"I'll stay! I'll get my horse and kill Jordan." Vicente headed down the alley towards the street. A cowboy rounded the corner and stopped short. The man pointed at them and yelled something, then ducked out of sight.

Brax reined up beside the kid. "All right, all right, we'll get the goddamn horse!" They doubled up on the mare and Brax urged her on. She thundered out of the alley and down the street. "You'll get us killed yet!" Brax shouted. They reached the saloon and Vicente leaned out of the saddle and swept up the reins of his horse. Gunfire erupted all around them and the roan followed eagerly. When Brax put his spurs to the mare they flew, raising enough dust for a cavalry troop.

Vicente twisted painfully in the saddle. He spotted a man in the upper window of the saloon raising a carbine to his shoulder. They were still within pistol range, but barely. It was an unfamiliar gun he jerked from the holster. There was no choice. A silent prayer raced through his head as he sighted and fired.

The man dropped the rifle, clutched his gut, and pitched forward. He hit the transom and was knocked back into the room. Red McKormick would never spend that thousand dollars. He lay at Harv Jordan's feet, bleeding crimson into the office carpet.

Jordan poked his head through the jagged pane. In the south the dustcloud was shrinking rapidly. He looked back to the dead bartender on the floor and dropped to his knees, seized him by the lapels and shook him as though to bring him back to life. And then, suddenly calm, he straightened and went about doing what had to be done.

The top drawer of his desk yielded a tablet of legal paper but he couldn't find his pencase. He slammed the drawer shut and pulled open a little-used side drawer that was crammed with old sketchpads. It stuck. He worked it free and dug his hands in. Among the papers he encountered a flat ungiving object, and gasped in recognition. As he extracted it a shower of old pen-and-ink drawings fluttered to the floor. He ignored them and held the portrait.

They stood in a lush Southern garden framed by live oak and magnolia against a backdrop of bougainvillaea. She in a white hoop skirt with sunbonnet and parasol, and beside her the young man—beardless, unscarred—wearing the uniform of a lieutenant in the South Carolina militia. On his mother's other side, *he* had stood—formidable and erect, brooding and beetle-browed. Although Harv had clipped him out of the picture a long time ago he could still see his father's huge shoulders—broader even than his own—and enormous head with its unkempt silver mane, precise square-clipped chin beard, massive brows, and relentless eyes the color of frozen nickel.

So many times he wished he could have excised Latimer Jordan from his life as he had from this sad portrait. But Harv's father was not a man to be eased out of the way. So imposing was he, in spirit as well as body, that he commanded a respect verging on awe. He was well-liked and admired by those who thrilled in the presense of power. But his son's earliest memories of the man were fraught with terror.

Even without his natural quickness of wit young Harv Jordan would have soon realized this gruff and insensitive bully was a poor candidate for filial adoration. Harv devoted much of his childhood to staying out of the man's way, and he was pretty successful at it. Until, that is, he reached early manhood and Latimer saw fit to step in and lend the guiding hand of experience in preparing Harv for a future befitting the last of the Jordans. To Harv, as his father never tired of pointing out, had fallen the task of carrying on the family tradition.

Not surprisingly this sudden interest in Harv's well-being exacerbated the already strained relationship between father and son. To the old man Harv's reluctance to attend the soldier's academy was heresy. Harv wanted no part of it. He just wanted to draw and paint. What was wrong with studying art? Cultural pursuits were not unheard of among Jordans. And then, capriciously enough, came the war. Only half-crazy dreamers were taken by surprise. Harv was one of them.

But not she. Not his mother. Months before the first shells landed on Sumter she began saving, secretly of course. Selling a patchwork here, scrimping on the household expenses there, even—the old man would have asked the Lord to strike him dead if he'd found out—digging into the tithe money. Saving for Harv's fare West. In those wild territories not much time and energy was spent worrying about the War.

But Latimer swore he'd sooner die himself and take them all with him than see his only son turn his back on their noble Southern cause. So young Harv Jordan did not go west in '61. Harv Jordan did not tame any wild, virgin land. Ill-suited as he was to brutish company and mindless obedience, Harv had a commission wangled for him in the army. The damned doomed Rebel army. He chose to face Yankee shrapnel rather than his father's wrath.

If the old bastard found Harv's reluctance to serve appalling he must have choked at the news of Harv's impending court-martial. For he never forgave, even though it happened at the war's end, when the remnants of that ragged army had disbanded. Harv's innocence or guilt were of no concern to the old man anyway. It was the dishonor of scandal that mattered.

And *she?* If it took the fall of the South to spring her son that didn't matter. Her prayers had been answered—her son was out of trouble. Harv told her, but not him, the whole story. Well, most of it anyway. Harv *was* guilty, and his only regret was that it had taken him so long to do it. And the lieutenant who had taunted him for so many months—Harv had long since been demoted to corporal—did eventually recover. All except for a slight limp and a shoulder that stiffened some in the damp, the way Harv heard it. She made him promise never to land those big fists on another man again unless his life was threatened, and, in a manner of speaking, he kept his word.

Now the awful war was over and he'd gotten through. Only now Harv was home again and the trenches of Petersburg were no closer to hell than this. Latimer hounded him unmercifully. Harv thought it must be his one joy in life, his purpose for being. Even though it made her so unhappy. It was their ceaseless bickering that drove her to illness, and. . .

For the most part she treated her disease as a minor inconvenience, and a temporary one at that. The fact was, they knew she was dying, the three of them, but never spoke of it. There was no denying her bravery; still, father and son made a concerted effort to avoid upsetting her. Of course she wasn't fooled. Their hatred lay silent and stinking like a dead thing under the floorboards. For Harv Jordan the prospect of leaving home again—of leaving *her*—was ghastly. The alternative, however, was unthinkable. Harv left Carolina forever.

It was to be only a respite. Shortly after Harv's move West the old bastard bought into a freighting concern in Denver. At first Harv thought he meant to run the new business by proxy. That was not to be. Harv was making plans to run again when, to his great surprise, he learned they were *both* coming. Even though she'd always said she'd never pick up and start over in the Territories.

She liked Denver, with its unexpected amenities and lovely scenery. But the doctors recommended a warm climate and the stern Colorado winters were too much. Latimer looked south for investments. He stumbled across the chance to buy a major share of an Arizona bank. She thought he signed the papers for her sake. Harv was sure it was a lucky coincidence, this Arizona deal. In any case it proved profitable.

With the new business came his father's offer of a job. He never for a moment believed the old man meant to bury the hatchet, though a position for Harv at the bank did make sense. He was skilled with figures, seemed to have the knack for guessing business trends—hadn't he saved the family from ruin in '73? Though the old man would sooner die on the rack than admit it. Harv was good with money. Working at a bank he could become even better.

But Harv balked at the offer, even when it was clear the old skunk would still be spending most of his time in Denver with the freighting line. In the end he accepted because of *her*. Because it pained her to see the two of them at such odds, because with matters smoothed between father and son she would know some peace in her last days on earth.

Harv started as head teller. The bank prospered. Harv was promoted to loan officer. For months he racked up a record of good accounts. Then one rather large loan defaulted and when they tried to foreclose they found the ranch in question was on government-owned land.

Latimer made a special trip down from Denver, and dismissed Harv from his post. However, Latimer stipulated, in a few weeks, when the present head teller moved, Harv could have his former job back.

Stunned by his blunder and his forced vacation Harv feigned illness and announced he was going to California for a period of recuperation. There he did, in a sense, recuperate—during long, enchanted, haze-filled nights on the wharf. What a glorious place, this honey-sweet San Francisco, with its foreigners and their fascinating vices! Never would he forget those swarthy mariners, oddly cultured and well-read, or the compelling Oriental gentlemen and their pipes stuffed with melliferous dreams. He returned to Arizona refreshed and renewed. Each spring, he vowed, he would return, to this seaport.

His mother had been dead more than a week when he returned. He awoke one dismal winter morning emaciated and sick in a Tucson hop den. He had to use the bank's name as a credit reference for stage fare back to Kingman. The next day he was back in his teller's cage. He learned that his father had personally filled in for him. Latimer left the moment the bank received the telegram from the Tucson stage depot checking Harv's reference. On orders from the old man no one asked him where he'd been. It was on this day that Harv started embezzling from his father.

He was careful. He took only a few hundred dollars the first month as he felt out the situation and hunted for new and better ways to make the records balance. And he was smart. He didn't spend his new-found fortune in any conspicuous manner. Some he stashed for future pilgrimages to the sea-coast. Some, but not much, he spent on opium. His pipe could take him far away and long ago and often *she* was there with him, which was wonderful; but always returned without her, which was horrid. So he quit the drug. A few days of hard drinking and the craving was gone. He'd killed it. Or so he thought. It was really only sleeping in a shallow grave. Some of the money he actually sent anonymously to charities. He didn't need the money so much as he needed the satisfaction of stealing it.

And then, as suddenly as a summer storm, the freight business collapsed. They'd weathered the depression of '73 but could not compete against the railroad. Creditors de-scended on Latimer Jordan. Harv would have relished the old bastard's predicament if it didn't involve an examination of all his assets.

Latimer had him prosecuted. His own son! Brought to judgment before the crude courts of that wilderness. Justice? *Revenge*. Revenge sanctified by the territorial court, meted out by the dreaded Yuma Prison, that den of filth and insan-ity, hellhole for murderers and highwaymen. Revenge. Not for pilfering a tiny percentage of the bank's considerable profits, but simply for being himself instead of a copy of Latimer Jordan.

He now knew he'd been fooling himself all along. He'd never really held the reins here. Such a chain of events could only have pre-ordained and he could no longer predict what lay in store for any of them. And a final chapter still re-mained. But Harv Jordan was no mere character in this tangled plot. He was a grand player in a mysterious celestial drama, the instrument, as it were, of a Higher Authority.

Gingerly he replaced the portrait and closed the drawer. In the drawer below he came across his pencase. He placed his finest gold point in the penholder and dipped it into the ink vial. "Last Will and Testament," he wrote. He'd been away from legal language for quite a while now, since his days at the accursed bank. Plain talk would be suitable. "I, Harv Jordan, do bequeath my property to . . ." and he stopped, pen poised over the paper.

Who indeed would mourn him were he not to return? *Was there no one?* There was one man, one who would miss him. ". . . Lin Hueng Chang of Salt Lake, Utah Territory." He put the pen down as if he were completing a physically exhausting task. What about his complicated outstanding accounts? Suppose Chang tried to collect? How many men would permit themselves to be driven off their land by a Chinaman? Most folks thought no less of killing a yellow man than a red one. And anyway, was it wise to leave behind so many who would curse your very name? There was a simple answer to all of this. He dipped his pen and wrote. "All debts, liens, mortgages owed to or held by me are forgiven, with collateral or property to revert to the debtors." He signed it and forged the name of Frank Tores as a witness. It was a simple matter to duplicate the man's childish block letter print. For good measure Harv backdated the document, scrawled a prominent "X" and printed Billy Ferson's name beside that.

He placed the will in his safe but left the door ajar. From the top drawer of his desk he took out his pistol and checked it carefully. Though he hadn't fired it in several years he kept it clean and well-oiled. Now he removed the sixth cartridge to avoid an accidental discharge and tucked the revolver into his belt. He walked out of the office to the landing and looked over his saloon one more time. Harv Jordan cleared his throat and assumed a dignified tone.

"Our town needs deputies," he announced.

A few hardcases threw down their cards and got to their feet. They had long since run out of money and were playing for each other's worthless markers. When Mr. Jordan needed deputies it meant there was killing to be done. And when there was killing to be done Jordan could be a very generous man.

There was no sign of pursuit, so Brax set an easy pace. He'd have to if the kid was to be worth a damn when the time came. Vicente made light of his wounds but Brax knew better.

"What a faint-hearted bunch of bastards. Think what I would have told them if they were Apaches!"

"What the hell made you think you could take them all on?"

"What made *you* think you could take them all on?" the kid fired back.

"I guess I wasn't thinkin'."

"And I am glad of it. But Tores, he still lives. And Jordan, he is a man possessed."

"Does seem that way."

"And I am tired of running low in the saddle, like a thief in the night."

"Does get stale, kid, I'll give you that."

"We must return now and finish this thing."

Brax had to laugh. "Mighty saucy for one who near got himself skinned alive."

But there was no reply. Brax turned in time to see him go limp, as if the air had been let out. Vicente slid from the roan and collapsed in a heap in the dust.


Starlight streaming through the big south window guided Benjy to the fireplace. He knelt and groped for kindling in the feeble light, then he lost he balance and toppled. He managed to break his fall with his hands and propped himself up again. This time he got a handful of twigs onto the iron grate. He found a match and lit the tinder. For a moment it seemed it would catch. Small, comforting flames licked the wood. He picked up a larger stick and dropped it in but succeeded only in scattering the twigs. He swore, pulled himself to his feet and reeled over to the table and found the bottle empty. He dashed it to pieces on the hardwood floor. He had begun the hunt for another when the kitchen door scraped the porch landing.

"Howdy, Benjy." The man stood framed by the doorway between the sitting room and the kitchen.

"Brax? Brax, that you?" Benjy stumbled towards the shape. "Kat, you there too? I did it for you, Kat . . ." he stopped. "It's no good," he mumbled, and turned his back and dropped to the floor. "Ain't it funny, Brax? More a man does to keep from losin' somethin', quicker it all slips away." He faced them again. "Goddamn I'm sorry, partner." He was on his knees. "You leavin', Brax? You leavin'?" But there was only the hollow silence.

"I ain't Brax," the visitor said. He pointed to his companion who had just stepped in. "And he ain't Kat. Can you guess who we are, Benjy?" Tores raised his Colt.

"Tores! What do you want here? Get out, get off my land, you maggot!"

Tores's slitted gaze narrowed even further. "Seems Mr. Thomas has had a change of heart about Braxton, eh Juan? It's just as well scarface decided to get rid of you, Benjy. Did you really think he'd give you this ranch?"

"Go ahead, shoot me down, you're still lower than buzzard shit! Go on, shoot! It'll be for the best."

Tores lowered the pistol. "You heard the news, Benjy? We have the Mex. Why, the boys are swappin' yarns with him this very minute. Fact, I'm missin' all the fun, jawbeatin' here with you."

"Burn in hell, Tores." Tores fired once. Benjy landed on his face, watched blood drip onto the polished oak floor, and died.

Kat had just topped the rise overlooking the house when she heard the single shot. Oh my God, was she too late? Had he taken his life? She'd come back, she had to be sure he was all right.

She heard only the sounds of the forest. No light warmed the ranch house and the front door stood wide open.

She slowed the pinto to a walk and drew the Winchester

from its scabbard, straining her ears in vain for any sound
from within.

Tores held his breath. The barrel of the rifle appeared and
slowly, warily, she followed it through the door. Tores
seized the muzzle of the gun. She gasped and her hands went
to jelly as he wrested the gun from her. In blind panic she
struck out and caught him on his sore jaw. He dropped the
gun and his hands flew to his face while she turned and ran.

To the barn and past it, across the high prairie not daring to
turn, her eyes glued to the wooded hills with their gulleys and
ravines that would stop a man on horseback. The hills were so
far, they shimmered in her tears, so damned far. Then she
heard it, above her sobs and her heavy breathing, the horses.
Their hoofbeats pounded the earth, grew louder by the second.

"Yeeeehaaaaah!!!!" The shrill cry of the hunter split the
night. Katheryn screeched and fell, she lay for a moment,
stunned, tasting blood where she'd cut her lip. The horse kept
coming, she looked up in time to see it, a monstrous steed
thundering down upon her. It was going to crush her!

At the last moment Tores worked the mount and it deftly
leaped over her. Tores spun it around and came back. Kat
was back on her feet and running.

"Run, little heifer!" Tores uncoiled his lariat from the
saddle pommel and twirled it over his head with a flourish.
Mondregas reined up alongside him and joined the chase,
laughing heartily.

She was too dry and hoarse to scream, her lungs felt as if
they would explode and sharp pains racked her ribcage. Only
vivid thoughts of falling prey to these dreadful men spurred
her on. Tores tossed the lasso. The rope missed.

The bandido cut her off! Mondregas's grin flashed in the
night. She'd never seen a horse so huge or a man with more
teeth. She cut to the side and he mocked her with his coarse
laughter. Tores reeled in the lasso and tried again. The coil
floated over her head and dropped. Katheryn was jerked to a
dead stop.

"Come along now, little heifer."

SLICKROCK RECKONING          163

The rope tightened as she fought. They took her back to the house at a trot. She stumbled and bounced, was dragged when she fell. Finally Tores marched her into the kitchen. "Juan, hide the horses," he barked.

Katheryn wriggled free and stood before him. Stay alert, stay calm, you may live through this yet. She took a deep breath. There may be things worse than death, she reminded herself. But not very many. How long before Brax arrived? How long could she hold out? If Brax arrived. . . .

"All right, Katheryn," said Tores. "Get us a light in here." Mondregas returned from the back where he'd tied their mounts. "Get us a light going, woman! I won't ask you again!"

She knew exactly where the lamp was, but fumbled endlessly in the dark.

"*Get that light!*"

Buy time, but don't push it, don't get them mad. They're murderers. "I found it." She lit the lantern and stared at the milky face of the intruder. Ferret eyes lost in a hatchet face. Frank Tores, killer for hire. *Sheriff* Tores, according to that ridiculous star pinned to his chest.

"I'm going to have to place you under arrest. For aidin', abettin', and harborin' a dangerous wanted man. Unless you change your ways and cooperate with the law."

"Where's Benjy?"

Tores screwed up his face. "I'm afraid he resisted arrest, Ma'am."

She glared at him, then strode briskly to the living room. They followed her to the doorway. She sank to her knees, cradling Benjy's lifeless head in her arms. The lantern in the kitchen seemed to halo him.

"You." She turned her icy eyes on Tores. "You filthy murdering scum . . . that poor weak fool, how could you . . . you filthy evil thing!"

"A lot of folks have been calling me names of late, and I'll thank you to hold your tongue. 'Less it's to tell me where Braxton is."

She stood, marched to within a foot of him and spat in his

face. Spittle and blood ran down his beak onto his chin. He slapped her hard.

"Ha ha, the bitch has *coraje!*" Juan Mondregas found it amusing. "How do you gringos say, 'spunk,' eh?"

"She do, don't she?" Tores wiped the mess off his face. He resolved to be calm. To give in to anger was to be weak, just look at Jordan. But he wasn't sure what was worse here, the woman spitting or that halfbreed animal laughing. "Now, Katheryn, are you going to tell me where he is now, while you're still nice to look at? Or later, when a drunk Navajo wouldn't want you? It's your choice, because you *are* going to tell me."

"Who's this Braxton?"

"Very amusing. You don't seem to understand. I can make things very unpleasant. Matter of fact there's a Mexican boy in jail in our fair town this very minute."

"Vicente!" she gasped.

"The point bein', Katheryn, my men and I sometimes get carried away. We've seen a few things during the Indian Wars and we are . . . impressionable, as Mr. Jordan might say."

"But why Benjy? Didn't he try to help you?"

Tores almost managed to look sad. "Ma'am, I must uphold the law."

"The *law!* Do you really think you're the *law?*"

"I really think—" he brought her face close to hers, within inches, and leered horribly—"I really think you're going to die most unpleasantly if you don't tell me where Braxton is."

# Twelve

"Gave me quite a scare, kid. Fact is you been givin' me scares since we met."

"Just a little dizzy. I'm all right now."

"Camp's just above the rise. Some grub will do you good."

They climbed the swell and rode through the tunnel of pine boughs that hid the little meadow. The fire smoldered bleakly and the bedroll lay where they had left it. Everything was the same, but no pinto stood in the shelter of the trees and no woman waited.

"They've got her! Oh my God, they've got her!"

Vicente was already on his knees scouring the ground. He found faint tracks in the spongy, needle-strewn earth. "Two horses. You and Katheryn, coming up from the ranch. . ."

"There." Brax indicated a muddled set of prints.

"No, those tracks are a bit older. But here—" His pointing fingers drew Brax's gaze—"your tracks, alone, coming to Lodgepole to rescue me." Brax waited. Vicente continued his study. "Ah!" he said with triumph. "The last set. One rider."

"Leading towards the ranch. . ."

"She must have gone back to Benjy Thomas, the traitorous swine who—"

"Yeah, yeah, save it." Brax stared dumbly at the tracks. "So she went back. Goddamn."

Vicente straightened. "We must be careful, Señor Brax, very careful. The whole town knows of your daring rescue, for which I thank you, and—"

"You're mighty damn talkative. What are you, practicin' up your English, runnin' for mayor of something?"

"It takes my mind off the pain, Señor."

"Sure, kid, I'm sorry. Let's hope everything's all right at the ranch. We'll fix you up proper and relax over a bottle."

"And el bastardo?"

"Don't you worry about Benjy. He'll be leaving."

Vicente pulled himself into the saddle. "I think the only way he leaves is on the wagon to the graveyard."

"You leave him be, Vicente. He's finished." For an answer Vicente let fly a vicious clump of spit. "I want your word on it. We're friends, right? Give me your word you'll leave him alone."

"Si, we are friends. And I give you my word. I protest, but you have my word."

"Good enough. Shall we ride, amigo?"

From the rise nothing seemed amiss. A light burned in the kitchen and the pinto stood by the front porch. "She's here! Thank God!" shouted Brax, but Vicente shushed him crossly. "You don't like the way it looks, do you, kid?" Brax whispered.

Vicente had tensed, seemed to swell in the saddle like a fighting tom fluffing out his fur. "I will not be surprised again," he said.

"What do you think, it looks too pat?"

"Does the lady Katheryn put her horse there, so near the kitchen? She did not when we rode in the other night."

"Maybe she would, maybe she wouldn't, but you're right. I'm not about to bet my life on it."

"I thought not. When I worked in the barn I saw that a good rifleman can send fire into the kitchen and the living room from the hayloft."

"All right, I'll light-step around back and see what we got here. If it looks like trouble I'll give a hoot."

"Now you are thinking like my uncle would. I am not so quick on my feet now but my hand and my eye, it is steady. I think."

"Well they better be. You see something that don't belong, drop him quick. Let's go."


Tores knew now it wasn't going to be as easy as he thought. Most women, they'd spill everything if you mussed their hair, let alone slapped 'em around. Not this one. Katheryn huddled in the corner. Her lip had split open again and was bleeding freely. A livid bruise swelled her cheek and threatened to shut her eye. Still she held out.

And Mondregas wasn't happy with this job. The portly Mexican had beaten many a whore senseless on hazy rotgut-charged nights and roared about it later, but this was different. This was a lady, and one with real spirit. And this Braxton must be some man to command such allegiance from a woman. Juan's look silently asked Tores to stop.

Tores did not wish to test the man's loyalty. "Juan, step outside and take a breather."

Mondregas stepped onto the porch, lit a smoke and waited for daybreak. Soon, in the east, the bellies of those clouds would bleed. And that kid in jail, he mused, he must be a tough one too, or we would have gotten word by now. I would like to know this Braxton, who draws so much sacrifice from those who love him. Too bad we are on different sides.

It was of course just a question of making a living. If Braxton offered work disposing of Tores and Jordan, Juan would consider it. As long as the pay was the same.

Tores knelt. "You can't hold out much longer, Katheryn. If we stop now, in a week or two you won't have a mark on you. If you let us stop. When Juan gets back, I'm afraid, we're going to start on the more permanent stuff." He looked her up and down, stretched his pale lips into a hideous grin. "Yessir, I believe we ought to take those clothes off. . ."

From Vicente's perch in the barn the stout form of Mondregas filled the doorway. Vicente poked the Winchester through the lookout and sighted down the barrel.

In the back of the house Brax came upon the two horses. So the kid was right again, Benjy and Katheryn were not alone, and Brax was certain these were no ordinary visitors. He crept to the back window where his eyes tracked the faint light that filtered into the room. There, by the table, were pieces of a broken bottle, and there, near the closed door that lead to the kitchen . . . Brax stepped back from the house and gave voice to the booming hoots of a horned owl. Then he tried the window. It was unlocked but stiff. He pushed and it moved with a groan. He ducked and waited.

The owl hoots didn't tell Vicente anything he didn't already know. From here the man in the doorway was a small target. A miss could mean the end of Brax and Katheryn. Even if he did drop him the shot would give them away. Vicente made his decision, and headed for the row of cottonwoods that stretched from the barn to the side of the house. He paused and gauged the distances to the watering trough ten yards from the bandido. The man was rolling a smoke, taking great care not to spill any tobacco. With an airy stealth and no more noise than the rustle of an owl's wings, Vicente crossed the narrow yard and ducked behind the trough.

He waited. Still the man smoked and stared at the dawn. Vicente worked his way along the porch. If the bandido heard him, or turned his way for any reason, he'd have to shoot him.

With a leap Vicente swallowed the last two yards that separated them. He knew where to hit, and he brought the butt of the pistol down hard. He caught the larger man under his arms and dragged him behind the trough. A search turned up a derringer. He pocketed it, then broke open the cylinder of the gunman's revolver and dropped the pistol into the watering tank.

Brax hoisted himself up to the window ledge and wriggled through. For a moment he hung there, then let himself down hands-first onto the floor. He got to his feet but in the dark he didn't see the bottle; and suddenly the floor rolled out from under him. The bottle scooted across the room and smashed violently against the stones of the fireplace.

At once the kitchen door flew open and Tores's gun spit lead, spraying hardwood splinters and riddling the walls. Brax hit the floor and kept moving, just to get out of the center of the room. He got off one shot as he rolled. It shattered the lantern on the kitchen table, plunging the house into darkness.

Labored breathing marked the seconds. Brax lunged for the kitchen. The blow to the chest knocked him over. He was on his back, dazed, when the foot came at him again. This time he got a hold of it and pushed hard. Tores flipped over backwards and landed with a crash somewhere in the dark kitchen. Brax scrambled after him, ready to throw himself on top of the man and beat or choke the life out of him.

"I've got a gun on the woman!"

Brax froze.

"Light a match. If you're holding iron she gets it!"

The first match spluttered weakly and died. Savagely Brax ripped another across his belt buckle, and a tiny flame glinted off the end of the .45. It was fully cocked, and pressed against Kat's temple. Her good eye still sparkled, and her split lip was twisted into a feeble little smile.

Vicente was the first to hear the riders. Half a dozen of

them, maybe, and they were just beyond the rise. If he was going to make it back to the house he'd have to break now, before they topped the ridge and had a clear view of the valley. Without wasting another moment he sprang from behind the trough. And stopped dead as if caught in a bear trap.

Mondregas clamped an iron grip on his leg, Vicente went for his pistol but a swipe of the big man's arm knocked it out of reach and suddenly the man was on top of him. He was forced to the ground, the massive hands digging into his throat. The weight was crushing, he couldn't kick, only pound weakly on the broad back. Desperately he groped for stones, anything, to crush the beast's head. The hands tightened, cutting off his air, and though he clawed wildly at the deadly vice he could not loosen the grip.


"Tores," Brax spat. "What slime brought you into this world?"

"The condemned man, defiant to the last."

"For God's sake, at least let the girl go."

"Certainly." He flung her to the floor. "She might have held out a bit longer for you, Braxton. But not much." He stepped away and backed towards the living room doorway. "Go to him, Katheryn. We're through with you now. Although Mr. Jordan will want his ranch back. Come to think of it, soon as I deliver your friend here, this ranch belongs to me."

She pulled herself to her feet. "I'd sooner see it burned to the ground."

Tores ignored her. "Tell me something, Braxton. Why did you do Jordan like that? What did he do? Cheat at cards? Mess with your woman? Ever seen him without the patch? You did a good job."

Vicente was going, fast. The world swam away and blackness floated in. Mondregas was ready to finish him off. He hoisted him off the ground like a goose-feather pillow.

It was a mistake. It gave Vicente room to get to his knife.

"Where the hell is Juan?" grumbled Tores. "Those greasers are all alike. Probably heard a shot and headed for the hills. Well, no matter. You know, Braxton, it's really too bad it had to be this way. Man with a shooting arm like yours, hell, we could have gone places together."

"No thanks, Tores. Man who lays in the sewer gets up stinking of shit."

"Too bad you feel that way. Man in my line can't help but admire the kind of work I saw back at the North Wash. Hell, you and me and that halfbreed . . ." He shook his head sadly. "Well, I expect Mr. Jordan will be anxious to hang you. Say . . ." he gestured towards the window with the muzzle of his Colt. "Speakin' of shit." The riders had cleared the rise and were cautiously approaching the house.

"Come on in, boys!" Tores bellowed. "I got him. I got the bastard! It's all over, Braxton, you've made me rich. I got—" But only a gurgle escaped his lips as Vicente jammed the blade deep into his spinal cord. Tores's gun dribbled from dying fingers. Vicente wrenched the knife free, swung his free arm around Tores's neck and sliced his throat from ear to ear. There was a sickening crunch as he hit the floor face down, but he was already gone.

"A man like him does not deserve to see his killer's face," Vicente said.

Katheryn retched. Brax shouted. "What the hell kept you?" He scooped up his Colt as the woman collapsed in sobs. He wanted to comfort her but this was no time. Vicente had just retrieved his Winchester when the first gunman walked through the door.

He waltzed in like it was Sunday meeting time, leaving the door wide open behind him. His gun was in his holster and his hands were at his sides, until his eyes fell on the stringless marionette that had been Frank Tores. Brax and Vicente fired at the same time, nailing him before he cleared leather. Brax kicked away the kitchen chairs and heaved the table over on its side. They had just ducked behind it before the sharp crack of gunfire shredded the dawn.

Bullets thudded to a standstill in the heavy oak, or ripped past them and smashed into the walls. The din of exploding shells pressed them helplessly behind the table. It couldn't stop the slugs for long, it was splintering badly and would soon split and crumble. Possibilities raced through Vicente's head. If that damned door was shut and bolted they could move to a better position, maybe even up the odds. But how could he move through this storm of flying lead?

As if in answer the firing trailed off. The horses were kicking up so much dust out there the riders could barely see the house. Brax popped up over the table and squeezed off two quick shots. To his surprise Katheryn appeared beside him working the lever of the Winchester and pouring bullets through the doorway. Vicente saw his chance and took it. He broke for the living room, dashed to the fireplace and threw himself in feet first. Andirons and ashes scattered.

It was a wide chimney and the stones were coarse and unevenly set. Arms and legs spread wide, he shimmied his way up through the open flue and out onto the roof. On hands and knees he scrambled up the slope towards the front of the house. The roof too had been neglected, he noticed, as cedar shingles flaked away beneath his feet. He reached the peak and below him the front yard was wide open.

A fresh barrage pinned Brax and Katheryn behind the table and suddenly a gust of wind came screaming out of the mountains and the swirling dust was snatched away. The men were in full view, nicely framed by the doorway. One of them leaped from his mount and dashed for the safety of the watering trough. Brax dropped him in his tracks. With their dust cover gone the men had their hands full working their milling horses to cover. Vicente tracked them with the barrel of his pistol, fired and watched a man plunge from the saddle. A rider turned and Vicente read the shock in his face as he spotted him, high in his deadly rooftop perch. The man raised his gun but Vicente fired first, and he too was blasted into the dirt. Another swung out of the saddle and Vicente fired once more, but the dust was up again and he couldn't see if he'd hit. Abruptly, horses began to emerge from the cloud at a dead run. Two riders had doubled up on one, leaving a horse dead in the yard. Vicente trained his gun on them but something kept him from pulling the trigger. Maybe something Brax had once said, he'd never know for sure. These men had had enough. They were running.

All but one.

At the instant of recognition Vicente gasped. It was a poor angle from here, the man was directly before the kitchen door and shielded from above by the porch roof. Vicente shifted for a better shot and hesitated, unsure—shouldn't Brax have him? But no shot sounded from below. This was no game and there might be no second chance. He cocked his revolver just as the shingles gave way and then he was sliding backwards. He grabbed the edge of the roof in time to keep from falling off and hung there, feet dangling over the backyard.

The sun topped the hills and bathed the ranch in the pinkish-gold, long-shadow light of morning. Brax emerged from behind the table and peered into the sun-streaked cloud, and then the dust parted and the big horse was coming at him. It seemed unable to turn. Not a fighting mount, maybe, or confused by the swirling dust and the close quarters of the porch where it now found itself, it panicked and reared back on its hind legs to its full height.

Open-mouthed, Brax stared at the rider towering above him. The man's head nearly scraped the high overhanging roof. He glowed in the dusty light of the new day, a bearded giant with an eyepatch. One eye bored into Brax and he was riveted, paralyzed by the apparition. From somewhere far away he heard a scream and then she was shaking him. At last he raised his revolver and fired. It clicked on an empty chamber.

Jordan got control of his horse and turned it. Brax seized the Winchester and got it to his shoulder, but he didn't fire. It was too late. Jordan was gone.


"I'm all right, Don. No worse than Ma used to get when Daddy'd come home drunk and dinner wasn't on."

"Where's your medicine kit?" Brax demanded as he set the table right. She pointed but Vicente was already emerging from the hall with gauze and disinfectant. "You too, kid. Got to clean those wounds good."

"You saw him, no?" Vicente asked her. "He is a devil who walks the earth."

"I'm going after him." Vicente started to speak but Brax cut him off. "Alone."

"What will you prove? I will only follow, so why the pretense?"

"You will not follow. You said it yourself—he is a man possessed. Do we leave her alone again?"

"Bah! He is a coward. He is back at the saloon. I know it."

"Ready to bet *her* life on it?" Vicente's expression did not waver. "Kid, please. It's my fight."

"It's crazy!" She slammed the iodine bottle down. "You must get to Moab, get the marshall, put a stop to this once and for all. If they put Jordan behind bars he can't send anymore men after us."

"Behind bars, Señora? On what grounds? Can we prove he hired men to kill us? I predict it will be most difficult."

Brax agreed. "Who would believe us? Me, just off Prison Hill, and a mongrel kid who speaks Spanish?"

"They'd believe me," said Katheryn. "I'd testify."

"Katheryn," said Brax patiently, "You ever see lawyers in court? Seen how they bend facts to fit their stories? They'd talk about your husband, say that Benjy was here right quick, and now us—do I have to spell it out?"

"Well goddamn it!" She grabbed a bottle off the shelf and

yanked the cork out. "This time you'll get yourself killed for sure! How long can your luck hold out?"

"Luck don't have much to do with it, Kat."

"That depends on who you mean by 'luck,' " observed Vicente.

"Enough jawbeatin'." Brax was on his feet. "You sure you're all right? Because I got to be going."

"No, I'm not all right with you goin' again, but I'd have an easier time turning a stampede with a corn shuck than changing your fool mind!" She stalked off to the table, found a glass, poured herself three fingers of bourbon and sat down. Brax nodded once at Vicente and left.

Vicente sat down across from her. "No tequila, eh? Well then, just one, perhaps. And then—" he pointed to the sitting room—"we must bury that poor fool in there. I have a prayer, Señora, it is for a man who feels great sorrow at the wrongs he has done. He dies before he can atone with deeds, but he is sorry, so he is saved. It is a beautiful song. I will teach it to you. It will make you feel better."

She smiled weakly and took his hand. "Thank you. I'd like to hear it."

"After all, the rites, they are for the dying, but the funeral, that is really for the living."

She stroked his slender hand. "You are a strange one, Vicente."

"What you need, Señora, what you need is for that man who just left to come back in one piece. Perhaps that is what I need most now too. But have courage, Señora. God has never left us. And now," he drained his glass and rose. "We have work. We must bury one with laughing eyes who broke. And then we must sweep away the scum so this ranch is sweet and clean again."

The early sun toasted his right side as he followed the well-worn trail to town. The morning mesa was bright with sound and color, a last touch of gaiety before winter set in for good. Brax heard the bubbly flute of a Western meadowlark, the whirring and clicking of the cicadas, and the drone of bees flitting among late-blooming firewheels and sunflowers. The sad *coo-ah coo* of the mourning dove floated from the low trees. It was Indian summer, and the sky said so too. Its bottomless blue was dotted with dazzling cottonballs which Brax knew but didn't quite believe were just big hunks of water and dust. Hell, this was no day to be riding off to shoot a man. The thought sent his hand to the reassuring grip of his Colt. Will the day ever come when a man didn't need to strap a killing machine to his leg when he stepped onto the trail?

Brax halted and climbed down. Ten yards away stood a clump of prickly-pear. He let his fingers dangle over the Colt, shook them to loosen them up. Aloud, he counted. On three he drew and fired. He missed the cactus pad by at least two feet.

Shaken, he reholstered the gun. Four years was a long time to be away from firearms, too long for a man who lived as he did. What *would* he do when he found Jordan? Shoot him in the back? Vicente had little compunction about killing like an Apache. And it was a damn good thing too, or Brax might not be standing here now. His Colt was in good order, reasonably clean; the holster was well-oiled and properly hung. So what was Brax going to do, take a week off and practice?

He closed his eyes and breathed in and out twice, deeply. Then he opened his eyes and drew. The boom of the shot seemed to reach his ears before he had cleared the holster and the cactus pad vanished, blown into dust. He tried again and another pad disintegrated. He missed his last target, the slender trunk of a pinyon tree, but not by much. Not by the width of a man.

Brax mounted up and rode on, his eyes raking the scrubby hills. It wouldn't do to be blasted out of the saddle now by one of Jordan's hired guns hiding in the brush. There couldn't be many more, not unless Jordan had collected every gunslinger in the three territories. After the beating at the ranch the last one was probably on his way back to Arizona, or wherever sane men didn't hire on to die.

*Sane.* Brax wasn't sure if Jordan could be put into that corral. A lot of men went a long ways to get what they wanted, but Jordan . . . Didn't he know Brax's death wouldn't give him back the eye? To Jordan, Brax was a ghost, and there were times when a ghost could be worse than a mere flesh enemy. Brax's death would give Jordan something back, something lost in those dank corridors that linked them.

Brax turned for one last look down the slope. There lay the ranch, nestled among gentle hills already ablaze with autumn foliage. Where he stood an arm of the sandstone desert reached into the mountains and the trail wound around a massive fin of layered, blood-colored rock. Once the ranch was out of view the trail climbed steadily until it was flanked by the dilapidated buildings of Lodgepole. This then might be his last glimpse of the place.

Had that been a fitting farewell? It was a fortunate man who found such companions in a lifetime. The bend in the trail was near, the point where the rise cut the ranch off. It wasn't too late to turn back.

That was impossible. There would be no peace for anyone near them as long as they both lived. Brax urged the mare to pick up her speed, as if by hurrying past the bend he could turn his back on cowardice, leave his fears here on this side of the hill. He rounded the turn.

Directly in front of him sat Harv Jordan.

Brax couldn't believe his eyes. Jordan's big horse grazed peacefully by his side while he sat on the rock, staring straight ahead. The Colt found its way into Brax's hand even as he marveled.

Here at six feet was the man. Somehow he had lost the eyepatch and the horrid crater gaped accusingly. Here was the face Brax had seen so many times in his nightmares, the brutal, hulking trustee who had had the run of the prison grounds; the man who had actually kept another prisoner—a mad, consumptive Papago—as his willing slave. Brax could see it as if it was last night, the glazed eyes of the stooped Indian, could hear his wracking cough as he followed Jordan like a hungry dog. Harv Jordan, whole and unscarred then. Somehow he'd grown into a huge, upright man with twisted desires.

"Will you have a drink with me, Don?" Harv Jordan said as he reached inside his coat.

"Hold it!"

Jordan opened his coat wide to reveal a pocket flask. "No gun." He uncorked the bottle and took a pull. "I didn't think you would drink with me. It's not written that way."

"What are you doing here?" He didn't really know why he was climbing down off his mount, but the pistol did not waver. "Why are you here? I don't understand. . ."

"We must not question these things," Jordan replied. The smile was an icicle shoved into Brax's spine, and now he was back, inside Prison Hill. Inside the hill itself, where prisoners picked and chiseled new cells out of the solid bedrock. Only feeble gray light filtered down to him. January rain wore the hill away even as he chipped at it from below. Brax didn't usually work alone, but on this day he did, and it was late. He was expecting someone to come and get him anytime now so he wasn't alarmed when the crazy Papago came shambling down the corridor. Brax didn't see the piece of tin clutched in his hands, the tin that once held beans but was now a jagged piece of rusting metal that could snuff a life as fast as a swipe from a sabre.

One moment he was setting aside his tools, the next he was in the grip of powerful red hands. One arm was locked around his neck, the other held the serrated metal up against his jugular. He was forced to his knees and out of nowhere came Jordan. He was huge. He brought his grinning face to within inches. The smell of prison moonshine was overpowering.

He stepped behind him, pulled Brax's ragged trousers down around his knees and stepped out of his own. . . .

On bad nights the sounds still came in the wind—the mindless, reedy gurgle of the Indian, Jordan's beastly grunts as he thrust, again and again until the Indian was wracked by a sudden coughing spell that doubled him over. He lurched against the stone wall and Brax seized the crude knife, twisted around and slashed out with all his strength. Jordan shrieked, stumbled outside, the Indian lay coughing blood in the dirt while Jordan flailed his arms and howled in the rain. . . .

"It was certain you were mowed down by the Gatling gun," Jordan said, as if they were chatting over morning tea. "Must you wave that pistol at me?"

"Yes." Then Brax heard himself say, "I wasn't in the break. I was in hospital with dysentery."

Jordan nodded. "I used to have such unreliable sources." He sighed. "Can you tell me what became of our friend? Oh I never could say the fellow's name—"

"The Papago died in the tubercular ward. Just after you left."

Jordan shook his head. "Ah well, the poor devil's probably better off, wouldn't you say? Say, isn't this nice? Two alumni meet to discuss their alma mater. So now what, Don? Do you execute me? Shall we duel, like gentlemen? Ten paces? No, let's draw, Brax. That is what they call you, isn't it? Yes, let's *draw,* like they do in dime novels people real back East."

"You're too pathetic to kill. . . ."

"Come on now, *Brax,* I don't know how this is supposed to end either. Neither one of us can change it. But of course you know that."

"You make no sense, but you listen to me. Leave Utah, forever." There was no change in the man's face. "I'm offering you your life, Jordan. I've seen enough killing."

"Exile? Like Napoleon on Elba, eh?"

"Whatever, but I'll hold you to it."

"Oh no, Don, that will never do. Perhaps I should at least consider it. I *will* consider it, if you put that pistol away."

"There are better ways of committin' suicide."

"Hah! Suppose I did draw on you? Don't you think you can beat me? You used to be quite a gunfighter, Don. What went first, your speed or your nerve?" He leaned forward slightly and bared his polished teeth. "You're afraid of me, aren't you?"

"You're goddamn right I'm afraid of you! Now what's it going to be? Make it snappy, the sight of you makes me sick."

"Well now, you may have had a little to do with that."

"No more talking. You going or dying?"

Jordan stretched the moment. "I've decided I'd prefer to live," he said at last. "I'll turn and ride."

"If I or Vicente ever see you again we'll kill you on sight."

"I understand. I will leave for good. However, you must put the gun away."

"I told you, that's out."

"I'm beaten, don't make me march at gunpoint. As a gentleman, as a son of the South, I ask you to let me keep my sword. Sheathe your weapon and you will never see nor hear of me again."

"All right, Jordan." Carefully he holstered his gun.

"Thank you, Mr. Braxton."

Brax didn't see it happen, or maybe he saw it the way a cat leaps across the corner of an eye. The coat was open and a hand blurred across Jordan's midsection and came up with a revolver. Brax watched. His mind had been wiped clean and his muscles didn't work. Jordan already had that canon trained on his heart before he could break the spell.

The Colt came up, faster than the thought, and Harv Jordan felt something thud into the right side of his chest and then he heard a shot. He couldn't muster the strength to pull the trigger of the gun he held. The two of them watched the spreading stain bubble up through his pleated white shirt. The pistol slid from his fingers. He opened his mouth to speak and toppled off the rock. Dust billowed and he was still.

Brax holstered the gun and walked the mare back to the bend in the trail. The land had never sparkled more dazzlingly. There would be no more backward glances. He mounted up and nudged the mare with his bootheels, and she trotted down the hill towards the big L-shaped ranchhouse.

# WESTERNS

## Nelson Nye

# Winners of the SPUR and WESTERN HERITAGE AWARD

Awarded annually by the Western Writers of America, the Golden Spur is the most prestigious prize a Western novel, or author, can attain.

| | | |
|---|---|---|
| ☐ 22767 | **FANCHER TRAIN**  Amelia Bean  $2.75 | |
| ☐ 29742 | **GOLD IN CALIFORNIA**  Todhunter Ballard $1.75 | |
| ☐ 47493 | **LAW MAN**  Lee Leighton  $1.95 | |
| ☐ 55124 | **MY BROTHER JOHN**  Herbert Purdum  $1.95 | |
| ☐ 72355 | **RIDERS TO CIBOLA**  Zollinger  $2.50 | |
| ☐ 30267 | **THE GREAT HORSE RACE**  Fred Grove $1.95 | |
| ☐ 47083 | **THE LAST DAYS OF WOLF GARNETT** Clifton Adams  $1.95 | |
| ☐ 82137 | **THE TRAIL TO OGALLALA** Benjamin Capps  $1.95 | |
| ☐ 85904 | **THE VALDEZ HORSES**  Lee Hoffman  $1.95 | |

Available wherever paperbacks are sold or use this coupon.

C-02

## J. R. ROBERTS

# THE GUNSMITH

## SERIES

An all new series of adult westerns, following the wild and
lusty adventures of Clint Adams, the Gunsmith!